DYLAN

LANTERN BEACH BLACKOUT: DANGER RISING

CHRISTY BARRITT

CHAPTER
ONE

KATIE LOGAN SIGHED as frustration mounted inside her.

Where were her lecture notes?

While other lecturers simply used their electronic tablets, she preferred paper copies.

She'd searched her office three times for her notes, and they were nowhere to be found.

She must have left them on the podium in the lecture hall after her last class.

With another sigh, Katie stood from her desk and placed her glasses on top of the piles of test papers she needed to grade. With nearly three hundred students, she *really* needed a new assistant.

As in, yesterday. She needed a new assistant *yesterday*.

The dean had promised she'd have one after

Addison had left for her maternity leave last week, but Katie hadn't heard a word since then.

Katie rubbed the skin between her eyes, feeling entirely more exhausted than she should.

Then again, who could blame her after everything that had happened this week? Everywhere she went, she felt like someone was watching her. Following her.

She glanced out the window behind her desk at the darkness outside. She'd worked entirely too late again tonight. She *had* to establish a better work/life balance. But since she was single . . . working was an easy way to fill her time.

Especially now that she'd discovered what had the potential to be an incredible story—one that could expose evil people for what they were and halt their plans.

But, first, she needed to retrieve her lecture notes.

Her heels tapped on the polished concrete floor as she walked down the dark, empty corridor of the University of Charlotte, where she was currently a visiting lecturer in their journalism school.

Since she'd been fired from Stone Media News as a TV reporter, teaching seemed the next best thing. At least, it allowed her some breathing room as she examined all her options.

But she missed being in the field. Covering wars. Riots. Conspiracies.

Teaching was just so . . . tame in comparison.

But it would be good for her to let some time pass. To let people forget about the debacle surrounding her being fired.

If only *she* could forget both the humiliation and injustice of it all.

She swallowed hard and pushed open the door to Pierce Auditorium, a two hundred-seat lecture hall.

Katie's hand fumbled along the wall until she found the light switch. A single bulb over the podium flickered on, and she stepped inside.

She walked across the stage and spotted her notes there.

Strange.

Katie wasn't forgetful, so it was unusual she'd left these. Normally, she wouldn't care. But it seemed as if her every action was scrutinized lately, and she didn't want to give anyone any more ammunition. There was nothing in her notes that should look incriminating, but the wrong person could find *anything* incriminating if that's what they were determined to do.

Either way, she'd grab them and then head home for the evening. Then she'd relax with a warm bath and the latest bestseller she'd picked up at the bookstore.

Just as she reached the podium, a sound at the back of the room caught her ear. She froze.

Was someone else in here?

The urge to run filled her. Katie was so alone in here. She should have turned on more lights.

But it was too late for that.

"Hello?" she called, hoping this was simply her paranoia at play.

No one answered.

Another shiver raced up her spine as she stared out at the auditorium. At the rows of seats where anyone could hide. At the darkness that would conceal anyone wishing to remain hidden.

Just as she grabbed her notes, another creak sounded.

Someone was *definitely* in here with her.

She quickened her steps as she headed back to the door.

As she did, a new sound cut through the silence. A click, followed by a whoosh. Then the faint sound of something clattering on the floor.

She gasped as she turned and saw a hole on the wall beside her. One that hadn't been there before.

A *bullet* hole.

Someone was shooting at her.

Using a silencer, most likely.

That clank of metal she'd heard? Had it been the metal casing from a bullet hitting the floor?

She sprinted out the auditorium door and ran toward the administrative wing where her office was located, wishing it was closer. Instead, it was on the other end of the building.

She glanced behind her as she rushed through the hallway, but it was too dark to see if anyone followed. Quickly, she pulled out her badge and swiped it in front of a card reader near the door.

The double doors buzzed, and she yanked one open and darted into the admin area.

Comfort filled her when she realized that only those with badges could get into the hallway after eight p.m.

Finally, she reached her office and slipped inside. With trembling hands, she locked the door, shoved a chair in front of it, and then slunk out of sight in the corner behind her desk—as far away from the entry as possible.

She grabbed her phone and dialed 911. While she waited for an operator to answer, she grabbed a letter opener from her desk drawer. She didn't have much to defend herself with, but at least this would be something.

She rattled off her information to the dispatcher

before ending the call.

Then she prayed the police would get here soon. She wasn't leaving this room until she knew the shooter was gone.

Who would want to hurt her like this?

Unfortunately, the list was too long to even begin to narrow down.

As more fear pummeled her, she gripped her phone and dialed her dad's number.

If this gunman found her again . . . that meant she might never talk to her father again.

The thought choked her.

As he answered, Katie cleared her throat. But her voice broke as she said, "Dad . . . I just wanted to let you know . . . I love you."

———

Dylan Granger readjusted his glasses before straightening the papers atop his desk.

In the distance, a door opened, and voices carried into the office.

"You hired a secretary without my input? I thought I would make the decision once you gave me the go-ahead. You should know by now that I'm pretty opinionated about these things."

A woman stopped in her tracks as she stepped

into the office and spotted him. Her blue eyes widened with surprise.

"I think assistant is the new buzz word." Dylan grinned before rising and extending his hand. "Dylan Granger."

The normally unflappable Katie Logan—at least, that was her reputation—observed him a moment, not bothering to hide her surprise before she shook his hand. "I'm sorry. I didn't realize you were already here and—"

"It's okay." Dylan waved her off. "I get it all the time."

She released her hand and offered a nod. "I'm Katie Logan. Nice to meet you."

"Same here."

She narrowed her eyes as she stood in front of him, clearly still trying to process his role here.

As anyone would.

Dylan didn't look like the type of guy who would be happy confined to a desk.

Because he wasn't.

He was a former Navy SEAL who'd been hired to guard Katie—only she couldn't know that.

After she'd been shot at, her father had offered to hire a security detail for her, but Katie had adamantly refused. That's when Richard Logan had contacted Blackout. Dylan had been assigned the job and given strict instructions to keep his real identity under wraps.

Mr. Logan had pulled a few strings, and now here Dylan was at the University of Charlotte pretending to be an assistant to intrepid reporter and visiting lecturer Katie Logan.

Katie continued to stare, her assessing gaze unapologetic as she shifted in front of him.

The woman was beautiful, with sleek blonde hair she wore pulled back in a low ponytail. Her makeup was understated and neat. She wore black pants with a light-blue blouse that showed off her slim figure. But it was her gaze that caught his attention. Perceptive. Curious. Smart.

"I hope you don't mind me being blunt," she started.

"I'd expect nothing less." Dylan had watched the woman on the news for years and knew she didn't hold back any punches. That quality had made her good at her job.

"This isn't politically correct by any means, but . . ." She shrugged. "I wasn't expecting someone like you."

"Tall, dark, and handsome?" He felt the twinkle in his gaze.

She narrowed her eyes again. "A grown man who looks like he should have far more experience by now than to want to be working as my assistant." She shrugged again. "I told you it wasn't politically correct."

"I appreciate candor. Can I get you some coffee?" he asked in an effort to play up her secretary comment.

Katie stared at him a moment as if trying to figure him out. Finally, her shoulders softened as she seemed to realize he was joking.

"Good one," she murmured. "And I can fetch my own. I don't expect to be treated like royalty. I mostly just need help with filing, grading, and managing appointments with students. Are you up for those tasks?"

"At your service." He offered a little bow.

"That's . . . cute." Katie's eyebrows pinched together as if she doubted her words. She sent him one more skeptical glance before stepping toward her office. "I have a class to teach, but we'll talk later and go over some more details. For now, just familiarize yourself with the office. Maybe glance over my course descriptions and curriculum to get an idea of what I'm teaching as well as my schedule."

"Of course. I'd be happy to."

She opened the door to her office and froze.

Dylan sensed something was wrong and edged closer. "Ms. Logan?"

"Someone's been in here." Her voice sounded thin, breakable, even though she held herself rigid.

Dylan stepped beyond her and glanced into the space.

A knife had been thrust into her desk, a paper impaled beneath it. Dylan pushed past Katie and strode across the room, his guard instantly going up.

He read the words written in red.

I tried to warn you to leave . . . You should have listened. Next time I won't miss.

CHAPTER
TWO

KATIE HADN'T HAD time to wait for the police to arrive. She had three classes to teach. Meanwhile, Dylan had promised to stay with the campus security officer to oversee the scene until police arrived.

She'd become a master at compartmentalizing. The skill had been necessary for some of the stories she'd covered, stories that had put her life in danger.

By her third class—the ethics of journalism—her mind was still wandering back to that knife.

How had someone gotten into her office? She'd been there early this morning before leaving to do some errands and attend a meeting. Dylan had told her he'd only gotten back from a college tour twenty minutes prior to her return, and that her office door had been closed when he arrived.

Speaking of Dylan . . .

His face flashed back into her mind. The man was tall and broad, with dark hair that curled on the edges. He wore a button-up shirt and a sweater vest along with oversized glasses and loafers.

She supposed, if she wanted to stereotype, he fit the academia look. But something about him threw her off balance.

When she'd asked the dean if she could hire a new secretary—assistant—she'd expected to choose someone right out of college or a grad student. Again, as another stereotype, Katie had expected to work with a woman. Not that she had a preference, it was just what she had anticipated.

She hated the generalizations embedded in her. But it wasn't so much those that had her bothered as it was Dylan himself. She'd learned to trust her gut instinct, and something told her the man was out of his element.

She wrapped up her final class of the day, snapped her binder closed, and clutched it to her side as she started off the stage.

As she did, she caught a glance of the patched but unpainted bullet hole in the wall.

From when someone had shot at her two nights ago.

She shuddered.

Whatever was going on here, she didn't like it.

Detective Morris had come after the incident in the lecture hall to take pictures and look at security footage. She hadn't heard from him since, though he assured her he'd look into it.

She didn't have high hopes he'd find anything.

"Excuse me, Ms. Logan!"

Katie paused on the stage as someone jogged down the aisle toward her.

It was Stiles Finnigan, one of her more inquisitive students. Something about his manner was off-putting, though she couldn't pinpoint anything specific. For some reason, dread filled her each time they spoke.

She plastered on a polite smile. "What can I do for you, Stiles?"

"I wanted to let you know that I really enjoyed your talk today. Thank you for being here at the college. It made my decision to attend UC even more of a slam dunk."

"I'm glad you're learning a lot." She shifted the binder in her hands.

Stiles always seemed to give her extra attention, almost as if he were starstruck. Normally, that wouldn't bother her. But considering everything that had happened, Katie was on edge. She seemed to look at everyone she talked to in a new light.

Until she knew exactly what was going on and who was trying to hurt her, that would continue.

That was probably why it wasn't fair to judge Dylan so harshly right now. She needed to find out his story before she jumped to any conclusions.

She would want someone to do the same for her, so it only seemed fair.

"I was hoping I could talk to you about an assignment I'm working on."

Tension crept up her spine. "I'm not sure I'm going to be able to fit you into my schedule this week. But early next week for sure. Call my assistant, and he'll set up an appointment. Or you could email me, and I can help you that way."

She glanced at her watch. It was getting late, and she needed to talk to her new assistant. She had to admit she was very curious to learn more about this man she'd be working with.

Even so, Katie was fully prepared to fire Dylan Granger if she discovered he wasn't qualified.

Dylan hadn't argued when Katie insisted on taking him out to dinner at a Mediterranean cafe on the edge of the campus so they could discuss his job.

In fact, the more Dylan could be with her, the

better. But he would have to be creative if he wanted to stay close. Katie Logan did not seem like the needy type, and that could be a problem.

Katie stared across the table at him, her perceptive eyes assessing him as she dipped a piece of pita bread into some hummus. They'd already discussed some of his duties in the office and her expectations of him.

She was direct, but Dylan didn't mind. That way, there was no confusion.

Her shoulders seemed to soften as the conversation turned more personal. "So, tell me about yourself, Mr. Granger."

"Please, call me Dylan. After all, I think we're the same age probably. Thirty-four? Thirty-five?"

She nodded slowly. "Something like that. But we're talking about you right now, remember?"

He smiled as he shoved a piece of grilled chicken from his kabob onto the white ceramic plate.

He'd rehearsed his cover story many times before this so he could keep the details straight. His colleagues had even set up some new social media accounts for him so if—when—Katie did any research on him, he would appear legit.

He tapped the table in mock thought. "Let's see . . . honestly, I'm not very interesting. I'm originally from Louisiana. That seems like a good place to start."

"I thought I recognized that drawl."

"I joined the military after high school, stayed in for about twelve years, and then moved to the Raleigh area. I worked in construction for a while but discovered I didn't really like that kind of job. I wanted a life change, so I applied at the university. Maybe I'll even go back to school eventually— though I'm not sure what I'd get my degree in."

Part of what he said was true. He really was from Louisiana. Really had been a SEAL for more than a decade. But he hadn't applied at the university to get a new job. And he'd left out the part about being a widower who'd been trying to piece his life back together after his wife's death five years ago.

He and Rachel had planned on having two kids by now and settling down for a somewhat normal life.

But things hadn't gone according to their plans— a reality he had to live with every day.

"And, in the meantime, you became a secretary— I mean, assistant?" Katie's eyes twinkled.

Dylan nodded, unfazed by her jab, which had no doubt been purposeful. "That's right. I'm enjoying it so far."

"So far, as in the eight hours you put in today?"

Katie squinted as she took another bite of her salad. "There's a lot more to the job than you might expect. I mistakenly thought I'd be in the loop on who was hired."

"I'm sorry. Somehow, I seem to have been fast-tracked. The dean said he has a soft spot for military veterans."

She frowned and tore off another piece of pita bread. "It doesn't really matter that much to me. After all, I'm only here for a year, and then I'll . . ."

Dylan watched, waiting for her to finish.

Katie wiped her mouth and shrugged. "Then I'll figure out what I want to do next."

"You'll go back to reporting, right?"

"It's complicated." Her voice sounded clipped as she responded.

Dylan had heard about the scandal surrounding her career, and he couldn't pretend that he hadn't. It seemed as if everyone knew.

But he wasn't going to bring it up.

Not yet.

Especially since he had more important matters to discuss.

He shifted in his seat, knowing he had to move beyond the superficial—but he had to do so very gently. "So that knife on your desk . . . that's got to make you feel uneasy."

Her gaze clouded. "It does. But I've never been one to back down to bullies, and I'm certainly not going to start now."

"If you don't mind me asking, why would someone be bullying you?"

Her expression stiffened. "When you're a reporter who's done as many stories as I have, there are a million reasons. A million people I've made angry. It's just a matter of the police going through each name until they find someone who fits."

He nodded slowly, trying not to appear overly eager to learn more. "I understand. I imagine that's a hard way to live. It seems as if you'd be on edge all the time."

Katie shrugged again. "I don't know about that. I really try to stay in the moment. That's what my dad always tells me is the source of being happy. Not dwelling in the past or jumping ahead to the future."

"He sounds like a wise man."

"He is."

Mr. Logan clearly cared about his daughter and didn't want to see anything happen to her. But the man had to get creative in order to keep her safe.

That's when Dylan had come into the picture.

Richard Logan was a former senator who now did motivational speeches for a living. He'd written three books and was a sought-after news commentator as well. His home base was here in Charlotte, although he often traveled.

The man was no stranger to hiring security, which was how he'd found Blackout.

Dylan had to wonder if Mr. Logan's residency here was one of the reasons Katie had chosen to take a job in this area. It made sense.

As they both finished eating, Katie began gathering her trash. "Anyway, I'm sure you have other things to do than worry about my problems, Mr. Granger."

"As I said before, please, call me Dylan."

"Very well, *Dylan*. I should let you get home. Anything else you need to know we can go over in the morning."

Dylan tried to think of an excuse to stay longer, but he couldn't come up with anything that wouldn't make him seem suspicious.

"Sounds good. For now, I'd like to walk you to your car." Before she could refuse, he added, "The social courtesy has been ingrained in me as a Southern gentleman. I hope you don't mind." He quickly stood, slipped his canvas jacket on, and left his empty plate and silverware in the marked bins near the trashcan.

She eyed him another moment before nodding. "If it makes you feel better."

"Think of it as one of the perks of having me as your assistant."

A few minutes later, they stepped from the restaurant. It was already getting dark outside, and the mild spring weather had dipped to a chilly forty-something degrees. The scent of garlic from the café filled the air as well as chocolate from a nearby candy store.

Dylan scanned everything around them as they walked.

His gaze stopped on a car whose headlights suddenly flashed on.

The next instant, the driver charged toward them.

CHAPTER
THREE

KATIE SAW the headlights getting brighter—closer—and gasped.

She knew she needed to move, yet her feet felt rooted in place as she stared at the vehicle.

Dylan shoved her, and the two of them tumbled onto a grassy median as the car sped past.

If he'd acted two seconds later, that driver would have hit her.

Katie's limbs trembled at the realization.

She also realized that her assistant was hovering over her, his strong arms and broad chest blocking her from danger.

She sucked in a breath as her heart released a surprising flutter.

She willed her body to stop. This was *not* what she needed right now—romance or even being attracted to her assistant were both bad ideas. *Terrible* ideas.

Dylan glanced down at her, still not moving away. "Are you okay?"

Katie nodded, even though she knew Dylan could feel her trembling. "I'm fine."

He rolled off her, stood, and then helped her to her feet.

"That was close." He studied her face as if concerned.

She wiped the grass from her clothes as she tried to gather herself. "I bet you didn't know when you took this job that you'd be throwing me out of the path of wayward cars, did you?"

She tried to add some lightness to the moment, even though she felt anything but calm.

"I'm not sure it was exactly in the job description, but I aim to please." He offered a fleeting grin.

Katie eyeballed Dylan again, still trying to figure him out.

He'd had quick instincts. Then again, he seemed both smart and athletic, so maybe that was to be expected.

Either way, she owed him a debt of gratitude. The man had saved her life.

She crossed her arms and ignored the stares of several people from the sidewalk in the distance.

No doubt they'd seen that whole showdown and were now curious.

Dylan grabbed his phone from his pocket and glanced at the screen. "We should call the police and report this."

"The police are going to think I have them on speed dial," she muttered.

He cast her a curious glance as he dialed. "The police, if they're worth their weight, should be on top of this. First, the knife, and now this."

Katie swallowed hard as she wondered how much she should share. She wasn't the type to blurt things. If she said something, it was intentional. She'd learned that skill through having a father who was a politician.

There was something about Dylan she wanted to trust. And the man had just saved her life . . .

She licked her lips. "And . . . I was shot at two nights ago."

Dylan's eyes widened. "What?"

Katie waved her statement off as if it weren't a big deal even though it clearly was. "I'm fine."

He lowered his phone a moment. "Do the police have any idea who's doing this?"

"Like I said, I have a lot of enemies. They just need to take their pick."

Dylan's jaw tightened as he shoved the phone to

his ear and talked to the 911 operator.

———

Dylan hated being deceptive.

But he'd been a Navy SEAL, and he knew that sometimes façades were necessary to get the job done. That's what he kept telling himself now also.

As he stood in the parking lot, he watched Katie climb into her car. The police—Detective Morris, to be specific—had taken their statements. He'd promised to look into what had happened as well as check security footage from local businesses and traffic cams.

Once Katie pulled out of her parking space, Dylan climbed into his SUV and eased out behind her, careful to maintain an innocuous distance back.

He needed to make sure she got home safely, but he didn't know her well enough yet to offer to drive her.

That meant he'd have to do things his own way.

The key was, he couldn't in any circumstances be caught.

He followed Katie as she left the university area and headed toward the suburbs. She owned a practical sedan, drove with a sensible level of aggressiveness, and didn't make any unnecessary stops.

Each of those things didn't surprise him, but he stored away the tidbits as he formed a mental assessment of her.

Finally, she pulled in front of a little cottage located in an older, well-established area of town. He was glad to see the porch light on and no large bushes or plants on either side of her front door that someone could hide behind. A single woman living alone couldn't be too careful.

Dylan cut his lights as he eased to the side of the road.

From a distance, he saw Katie climb from her car and glance around.

She was nervous also.

Good. That would keep her sharp. It was easier to guard a fearful person than to guard someone who arrogantly thought they were untouchable.

Katie quickened her steps as she hurried toward her front door. A moment later, she scrambled inside.

Dylan pulled back onto the road and stopped across the street, one house down. He hoped to blend in with the other cars on the block. But he needed to be close enough to see her yard.

Later on, he'd call Colton Locke, his team leader, and ask if they could put another agent on duty in the evenings.

With everything going on, Dylan wanted eyes on Katie at all times.

Just in the past two days, she'd been shot at, almost run over, and a knife had been left on her desk.

Someone wasn't playing games anymore.

Katie hadn't told her father many details about what was going on—only that she'd been shot at. Whatever had triggered this, Katie was keeping it under wraps.

She knew more about who might be behind these events than she was letting on. Dylan was nearly certain of it.

For now, he settled back in his seat so he could be on the lookout for trouble.

KATIE TURNED on the bath water, added some bubbles, and then waited for the tub to fill.

She wished taking a nice warm bath would melt away all her worries. That clearly wasn't the case. Still, she was willing to give it a shot.

She was jumpy. Even she couldn't deny that. She thought of herself as being tough, but that didn't mean she didn't feel afraid at times.

As soon as Katie had stepped inside, she'd taken the gun from her purse and had searched her entire house.

She had a concealed carry permit, but she rarely took her gun with her.

At least, she hadn't until she'd been shot at two days ago.

She wasn't the type who wanted to wait for

others to keep her safe. But, tonight, part of her had wondered what it would be like to have someone watch her back. Maybe she shouldn't have refused her father's offer to hire round-the-clock security for her.

As the scent of lavender filled the room, Dylan's face appeared.

He had watched her back tonight. He'd seemed quite adept at it too.

Katie quickly chided herself. Why in the world was she thinking about Dylan again? It didn't make any sense.

Yet his face remained in her mind.

She'd always liked a good mystery, and Dylan seemed *exactly* like one of those.

He was someone she'd love to unravel. She wanted to hear more of that Louisiana accent. Learn what had really brought him to the university.

Not that being an assistant wasn't an admirable job. But he seemed like the type who was capable of doing much more. Like a leader—a strong, quiet leader.

With a broad shoulder she could lean on.

Katie sighed. That thought was definitely inappropriate. Dylan worked for her. The idea of striking up any type of relationship should be off limits.

She shoved those possibilities out of her mind as

she twisted her earrings from her ears and placed them in her jewelry box.

For so long, she'd been perfectly content to be married to her job and to be alone. Sure, she'd dated some. A few times she'd even dated seriously. But nothing had worked out, and none of those relationships had left her heartbroken when they'd ended.

Probably because she was in love with her work.

The problem was—did her work love her back?

She shook the thought from her head before turning off the water and dipping a hand in to test it.

Perfect.

Katie climbed into the tub and let the warmth surround her. She closed her eyes, attempting to relax, but it didn't quite work. Keeping her eyes open seemed like a much safer option.

She'd been in the tub less than five minutes when a noise caught her ear.

She sat up, the hair on her arms rising.

Was she imagining things? Or had one of her windows just rattled?

Quickly, she scrambled from the tub, pulled her robe on, and grabbed her gun.

Her hands trembled as she paced toward the bathroom door.

What if an intruder was in her house?

———

As Dylan saw a shadow move near Katie's house, he lowered his phone.

"Colton, I'm going to have to call you back," he quickly muttered.

He shoved his phone back into his pocket and observed Katie's place more closely.

He thought for sure he'd seen a figure moving near the flowerbeds.

He'd been keeping his eye on the front, and no one had approached her house from that direction. But someone could have used a different route to enter the backyard.

His muscles tightened.

Wasting no more time, he crept from his SUV and headed toward Katie's house.

There it was.

The shadow.

A man wearing all black.

The trespasser stood outside of Katie's window, reaching up as if trying to get inside.

"Hey!" Dylan yelled.

The man froze before bursting into action and taking off in a run.

Dylan remained on the man's heels.

He desperately wanted to see who had been lurking outside her house.

But the man was fast—faster than Dylan had anticipated.

The man in black rounded the corner to an adjacent street. The next instant, he jumped into the passenger side of a dark vehicle idling near the curb. The driver squealed away.

Dylan squinted, trying to get a look at the license plate. But it was no use. It was too dark, and Dylan was too far away.

He paused on the sidewalk, his hands on his hips as he drew in deep breaths.

That guy hadn't gotten inside Katie's house. That was the good news.

The bad news was that he'd tried to get to Katie.

That was three encounters in one day.

The knife in the desk. The near hit-and-run. And now this.

Someone was desperate to get to her.

Tension rising to new levels, Dylan strode back to his car.

It looked like he'd be staying here tonight. The task would make for a long day tomorrow, but knowing that Katie was safe would be worth the trouble.

AS KATIE WALKED into work the next day, she felt the dark circles beneath her eyes. Felt her steps drag. Felt the sluggishness trying to claim her thoughts.

She'd hardly gotten any sleep last night.

After she thought she'd heard someone outside her house, she'd propped herself against the wall with her gun in hand, just waiting to hear something else.

She thought she'd heard a shout.

Perhaps from one of her neighbors.

Then nothing.

But she hadn't slept. Instead, she'd waited on edge.

Thankfully, the rest of the night had been quiet.

Today, however, her sleepless night was already catching up to her.

Dylan looked up when she walked inside, and a bright smile lit his face. He slipped on his oversized glasses and, for a moment, reminded her a bit of Clark Kent.

Was Dylan really Superman in disguise?

Katie nearly laughed at her own observation. But there *was* something about Dylan that reminded her a little bit of the seemingly meek to secretly mighty type.

"Ms. Logan, how are you this morning?" Dylan rose and presented her with a cup of coffee. "I know you don't expect coffee handed to you, but this is voluntary on my part. One sugar, one cream. Professor Lyndell told me you like it that way."

"Major bonus points for this." Katie took a sip before nodding. "I'm tired but okay."

He tilted his head before crossing back to the other side of his desk. "You didn't sleep well?"

"No, not really." She stepped toward her office, not offering any other details.

"I've been here for the past hour. I was awake early, so I decided to come in and get a start on some filing. You'll be happy to know no one has gone through your office since yesterday. Before we left, I put a piece of tape near the top of the door. It was still intact this morning."

That did make her feel better to know no surprises were waiting for her inside.

She cast him a glance and nodded. "Thank you."

"Anything specific I need to know about today?"

"I have one class at eleven, another at one, and one at three. In between, I'll be meeting with some students about their class projects. If you could help me schedule some meetings for next week, it would be great."

"I'd be more than happy to."

With one more glance at him, Katie slipped into her office.

Almost as soon as she shut the door, her phone rang. It was Connie, her cousin who lived in Asheville. Connie worked as the office manager at Baylor Beauty and had suspicions something was going on at work—suspicions she'd shared with Katie.

Katie had always felt protective of her younger cousin. Ever since she'd caught some other kids bullying her in sixth grade, Katie had become her unofficial protector.

"Hey." Katie held the phone to her ear. "What's going on?"

"Hey, cuz. I'm calling to check in. Anything new

with your investigation? Did you find anything out yet?"

Katie glanced at the door, making sure it was completely closed, and lowered her voice. "I'm still digging, but I don't have anything to report yet. Any updates on your end?"

"There's lots of whispering here at the office—especially whenever Kingston Baylor is around."

Katie's lungs tightened. Kingston Baylor was the entitled son of Earl and Wanda Baylor, the founders of Baylor Beauty, a manufacturer and supplier of products to salons around the country.

The man was trouble. Katie had looked into his background, but she hadn't discovered proof he was doing anything illegal. Not yet.

Connie was certain that he was.

"Don't ask too many questions," Katie warned her. "I don't want you to get hurt."

"I know. I won't. It's just . . . I know something is going on here. I'm pretty sure Kingston is in the middle of it. I feel unnerved every time I see that man." Connie's voice wavered.

"Then stay away from him. Let me do the dirty work." Katie had experience with this kind of research. She knew how to find answers without raising suspicions.

"I don't want you to get hurt either," Connie murmured.

Dylan's picture again flashed through her mind. Which was ridiculous.

Katie certainly wouldn't count on her assistant to protect her.

She'd do just fine on her own. Going at these things by herself was the safest bet. Depending on others would just disappoint her in the end. It always did.

"I'll be okay," Katie insisted. "I promise. As soon as I know something, I'll be in touch."

Katie didn't tell her cousin that ever since Katie had started looking into missing supplies at the warehouse there had been attempts on her life.

That's why Katie wondered just what the company was covering up.

The components of beauty products could be used to build bombs.

But she couldn't go to the police with this information until she had solid proof. Otherwise, she truly would be putting her cousin in danger. Plus, after the debacle that had cost Katie her job, everyone seemed cautious around her. She suspected the police would be no different.

Doubt had been planted.

Just as Donovan Sullivan had wanted.

Anger still burned through her at the thought.

That's why Katie had to plan each move carefully.

Very carefully.

———

Dylan had been keeping a close eye on things all day, but thankfully there hadn't been any trouble.

He'd remained in his car outside her house all night until Maddox King, another Blackout agent, had arrived to take his place. Dylan had hurried back to his apartment with just enough time to shower and change before heading into the office for the day.

He'd wanted to arrive early to check things out and get a scope of the place.

All day, he'd monitored everyone who came and went. He'd checked Katie's emails—at her request. He'd studied her schedule.

Toward the end of the day, he'd walked Katie to one of her lectures under the guise of learning more about her job. She seemed to buy the excuse.

As he stood in the back of the lecture hall listening to Katie talk about interview techniques, a man stepped in and stood beside him. The man was tall and lanky, with wire-rimmed glasses and short brown hair. Probably close to forty, if Dylan had to guess.

After a moment, the man extended his hand. "I'm Waylon Sears, the Dean of Students."

"Dylan Granger. Nice to meet you." The Dean of the School of Journalism had hired Dylan, so he'd never met Waylon before.

Waylon nodded. "That's right. You're the new hire in the journalism department."

"That's me."

"Somehow, I expected you to be younger, even though I did look at your résumé. How do you like it here so far?"

Dylan nodded at Katie as she spoke from the stage. "Ms. Logan seems like an incredible teacher and journalist."

Waylon's face practically beamed. "She's one of the best. We're all thrilled to have her here this year. I was nervous that what happened at her previous employment would stain her reputation. But that doesn't seem to be the case. The students still respect her."

"All of them?" Dylan tried to keep his voice casual so he wouldn't raise suspicions.

Until Dylan knew what was going on, he needed to keep his eyes open to all the possibilities of who could be behind these attacks.

A student? Another jealous faculty member? Someone Katie angered through a past exposé?

There were almost too many possibilities.

The dean's gaze darkened as if he didn't appreciate Dylan's prying. "Yes. I've been very happy with the response."

Something about his words didn't ring quite true. Dylan felt certain this man had faced some backlash because of Katie's presence here. But Dylan knew better than to push any harder.

Waylon looked away and sneezed. "Excuse me. Allergies at this time of year . . . they can really make a person miserable."

"Bless you," Dylan said, deciding to play things cool.

"I hope you enjoy working here." Waylon stepped back and sneezed again. "I've got to get back for another meeting—after I grab some tissues."

As the man walked away, Dylan wondered just what he was hiding.

The way Waylon looked at Katie made it clear the man admired her.

Was that where his revere stopped?

Dylan turned back to Katie.

Just how deep did that admiration go?

CHAPTER
SIX

AS KATIE WALKED beside Dylan back into her office area, she stopped in her tracks at the figure she saw waiting there.

The man was only five foot ten, but he carried himself like a giant. His hair had prematurely turned gray when he was only forty, but now at sixty-one his skin was still smooth and unblemished. His smile lit up rooms, and his charisma drew people to him like flies to sugar.

"Dad?" she murmured.

Her father turned and a bright smile lit his face. "Katie girl!"

She gave him a quick hug and a kiss on the cheek.

Whenever her father was around, Katie felt like a little girl again. Most of the time she reveled in the feeling. Her dad always made her feel safe and protected. He'd encouraged her that she could do whatever she set her mind to. He'd pushed her toward her dreams and supported her when she'd fallen short.

But what was he doing here now? He didn't often pay her a visit at the university.

"I happened to be in the area, and I hoped that you might be done teaching for the day. I thought I'd see if you wanted to do dinner." Her father seemed to read her mind. His gaze shifted beside her to Dylan. "Who is this?"

Before she could answer, Dylan extended his hand. "Dylan Granger. Her secretary. It's nice to meet you."

Her father's eyebrows shot up. Katie knew by the look in his eyes that he was curious about her newest hire.

"He's my new *assistant*," she quickly said. "He just started yesterday."

"Just yesterday? Are you new in this area?" He turned inquisitive eyes on Dylan.

"As a matter of fact, I am. I'm from Louisiana."

"Great state. You an LSU fan?"

"Go, Tigers . . . what kind of Louisianian would I be if I weren't?"

"How about that crawfish etouffee?" Mr. Logan

rubbed his belly as a look of delight took over his face.

"I can make up a mean dish of that," Dylan said. "You let me know the next time you want some, and I'm your man."

"It's a deal." Her dad chuckled before turning back to Katie. "I like this guy. Let's bring him with us."

Katie started to object, but before she could, her dad put one hand on her back and the other on Dylan's shoulder. He directed them to the door.

That was her dad for you. He had a way of getting what he wanted and being nice about it. It was probably why he'd successfully run for office and served as a senator for nearly two decades.

It looked like Katie was going to continue getting to know Dylan Granger even more . . . whether she wanted to or not.

———

Dylan couldn't help but marvel at how Katie's father was better at pretending than he'd ever imagined. No one would have guessed the two men had already met each other and that, in fact, Mr. Logan had set all of this up.

The man was a good actor. Then again, he was a politician so maybe that was a given.

Dylan preferred having his own vehicle at his disposal, so he drove separately to the restaurant. As usual, he scanned everything around him as he traveled, looking for any signs of trouble.

He saw nothing.

But having Katie at dinner with him along with the former senator and current political commentator? That was just ripe for trouble.

The good news was that Maddox was now here to help. At least Dylan might get some sleep tonight so he could be at his best.

A few minutes later, Dylan pulled into a space in front of Dark House Tavern, an upscale European-style restaurant. As soon as he stepped from his SUV, the scent of fried fish and sizzling meat filled the air.

"I highly recommend the Beef Wellington," Mr. Logan said before pinching the tips of his fingers and thumb together and kissing them. With a flair of his fingers, he tossed the kiss into the air. "It's absolutely fantastic."

"I personally like the bangers and mash—but only when I want to splurge," Katie added.

Dylan smiled. "I'll take both of those into consideration."

"Now, let's get inside." Mr. Logan nodded toward

the front door. "I already made reservations. If there's one thing you might learn about me, it's that I hate waiting."

It wasn't until they were inside, seated, and had ordered that the conversation shifted from small talk to something more personal.

"I just have to say—I can truly admire a man who embraces what he wants to do and doesn't care what other people think." Mr. Logan nodded as he observed Dylan.

Dylan leaned back in his seat. "That's me."

He wasn't sure that was totally true. Dylan had wanted to be a Navy SEAL since he was a child. As soon as he was out of high school, he joined the military and had eventually been accepted into BUD/S.

He'd worked hard to finish training, and then he served as a SEAL until he'd known it was time to get out.

Joining Blackout seemed like the next best thing because Dylan still got to use his tactical skills, just in a different environment. Plus, he got to work with some of his former colleagues—the best in the business and some of the most honorable men he knew.

"Did you know that my daughter has won three George Polk Awards and was nominated for a Pulitzer and a Peabody?" Mr. Logan started, a spark of pride in his gaze.

"As a matter of fact, I did hear that." Dylan glanced at Katie, who rolled her eyes to the side as if embarrassed. "I used to watch you on the news. I always enjoyed your coverage."

Katie appeared to blush as she sat across the table from him. "I enjoyed doing my job. Now I hope I can teach others to be strong, ethical journalists who present both sides of the story."

"Unbiased?" Dylan added, taking a sip of his water.

Katie shrugged, seeming totally at ease with the conversation. "I don't believe there's any such thing as unbiased. All we can do is present both sides. But our true feelings always emerge in some way, whether we intend that to happen or not."

He nodded as he listened to her explanation.

"What about you?" Mr. Logan turned back to Dylan. "Tell us about yourself. Are you married?"

Dylan felt his smile slip. "No. But I was."

"Divorced?"

His throat burned. It was still hard to talk about what had happened. Rachel had been a wonderful woman . . . until a man named Brian Abrams had wanted a quick drug fix and decided Rachel's life wasn't worth as much as the contents of her wallet.

Dylan cleared his throat. "Actually, Rachel died five years ago."

Katie's eyes widened. "I'm so sorry to hear that."

Dylan nodded, not wanting to get into it. Even though time had passed, it still hurt to think about his loss. "I appreciate that, Ms. Logan."

"Katie . . . please, call me Katie. At least, outside the office."

He nodded. "Okay. Thank you, Katie."

Thankfully, the bread was served just then.

It was the perfect excuse to change the subject.

KATIE COULDN'T GET Dylan's words out of her head.

His wife had died.

She wondered what happened and how all that had possibly led him to the point he was at right now —in his mid-thirties working as an assistant at a university in a field he had no experience in.

Katie had always been curious. Probably too curious. It was part of the reason she'd become a journalist—so she could satisfy some of that curiosity.

But she knew better than to ask more questions. She knew by looking at the grief in Dylan's eyes that he didn't want to talk about this anymore, and she couldn't blame him.

The rest of dinner, the conversation was light and pleasant. Katie's dad was always entertaining.

Several people recognized him and stopped by the table to strike up conversations. When they did, Katie turned away so they wouldn't see her and ask her questions also.

That had been Katie's life for as long as she could remember. She didn't even mind the interruptions—not usually, at least.

With her dad preoccupied, Katie's thoughts wandered to her conversation with Connie earlier today.

She didn't want Connie snooping around. As soon as Connie had told Katie about her discovery, Katie had started investigating and asking questions. That's when the trouble had begun.

Katie had a feeling that whatever was going on with the beauty company was big time. She'd done her research, and she knew that acetone and peroxide-based bleaching formulas could make TATP. Bombs. Explosives.

"Let's order dessert." Her dad's voice cut through her thoughts. "I insist."

Katie wasn't going to argue.

Just as they picked up the dessert menu, a terrible sound filled the air outside.

Metal crunching. Brakes squealing. People screaming.

As Dylan jumped to his feet, Katie's heart pounded in her ears.

Just what had happened out there?

———

"Stay here," Dylan ordered before rushing toward the front of the restaurant and throwing the door open.

His eyes widened when he spotted a car squealing away from the parking lot.

As he glanced back, he saw Mr. Logan's BMW.

The rear looked like an accordion.

Someone had smashed it and fled, hadn't they?

Another message being sent, no doubt. This couldn't be a coincidence.

Mr. Logan and Katie both rushed outside.

"What's going on?" Mr. Logan's deep voice rumbled through the air.

They followed Dylan's gaze and saw the car.

The father and daughter froze.

"The driver just kept going," a witness said. "It was almost like he panicked."

Or the driver had *meant* for it to happen, Dylan thought to himself.

"Oh, Dad . . ." Katie put her arm around her father and leaned into him.

"I can replace cars. I just hate the senselessness." He frowned before rubbing a hand over his jaw.

Dylan could understand the sentiment. All too well for that matter.

He started to grab his phone to dial the police when sirens sounded in the distance. Clearly, someone else had already called.

Dylan glanced at the onlookers around him, searching for a sign of anyone suspicious. But the people on the sidewalk appeared innocent.

"Was anyone able to get a license plate?" he asked the crowd.

The witnesses all shook their heads, looking mostly dazed. No doubt they had been enjoying a nice evening out when this occurred.

Dylan knew one thing for sure. Someone was still trying to send a message.

This person wouldn't stop until he got what he wanted, would he?

CHAPTER
EIGHT

KATIE'S GUT churned with worry as she stared at her father's damaged car in the parking lot while the police took their statements.

Someone had clearly been trying to send another message.

It had worked.

She wasn't the only one in danger.

So was her father.

Unless she backed off.

She hadn't even discovered that much yet. She'd simply looked into Kingston Baylor's criminal history. She'd tracked the man's schedule. Put together a timeline, noting when he'd been out of town. Tried to figure out possible connections.

If Kingston truly was stealing caustic substances —if that's what was in the bottles Connie had seen him taking—then what was he doing with it? Was it selling acetone to someone who might want to use it for nefarious purposes like bombs?

Katie had hoped if she continued to track the man, she might discover what he was up to.

Bombs were nothing to play with.

Her father turned toward Dylan. "I need you to get her home for me."

"Dad . . ." Her cheeks flushed as she dropped her head to the side.

Though she appreciated the fact her father had always been her guardian, sometimes he took things too far.

Like now.

She didn't need her new assistant babysitting her.

"After everything that's happened, I won't be able to rest until I know you're somewhere safe." Her father looked back at Dylan, worry filling his gaze. "So, will you do it for me? Drive Katie home and make sure she gets inside safely?"

Dylan didn't hesitate before nodding. "Of course."

"I'll have Danny come and pick me up." Danny was her father's right-hand man at his office.

"Are you sure we can't stay here with you?" Dylan shifted, his hands on his hips as he became all business. "I don't mind."

"I don't mind either." Katie hated to leave her father alone to handle this mess.

"It's getting late. I insist that you guys go home. I just need to know my little girl is safe."

"Dad . . . I'm hardly a little girl anymore."

He gently patted her cheek as his affectionate gaze met hers. "You will always be my little girl."

Katie wanted to be irritated, but she couldn't be. She knew her father loved her. Her mother had left when Katie was only two, abandoning them to start a new life in California. Last Katie heard, her mom had a new husband and three other children.

Her mom had made no effort to contact Katie in more than thirty years.

So, for what seemed like forever, it had been only Katie and her father. The two of them were close and had dinner together at least once a week, if not more. They talked on the phone almost every day.

Dylan pointed to his SUV, which was untouched by the hit-and-run. "Are you ready to go?"

Katie nodded, knowing better than to argue any more. "But I want to pick up my car. I don't want to be stranded at my house without a way to get to work tomorrow."

"Understood."

Surprisingly, Katie was looking forward to talking

to Dylan more. The man was fascinating . . . but she also reminded herself not to get too close.

———

Dylan gripped the steering wheel as he and Katie headed back to the university in his SUV.

"I'm sorry that my father asked you to do this," Katie murmured beside him.

Dylan glanced at Katie and shrugged. "He is just trying to watch out for you."

"He still acts as if I'm only a child sometimes. But I suppose it's sweet."

"I can tell he loves you and would do anything for you. There are people in this world who dream about having someone in their life who cares for them that deeply."

A frown flickered across her lips. "No one can argue with that. He really wanted me to take this job in Charlotte so I could be close to him."

Dylan stole a glance at her. "Do you miss New York and traveling the world?"

Katie seemed to think about it a moment before shaking her head. "I thought I would. But I don't really miss the traveling. I just miss the stories. They were the whole reason I traveled in the first place. So

I could listen to people. So I could speak for the helpless."

"Sounds noble."

"But then . . . then Donovan Sullivan happened."

Dylan knew what she was talking about, so she didn't need to explain.

Donovan Sullivan was a business mogul who owned more companies than Dylan could count. He'd started in the insurance industry and had moved on to buy a professional football team. After that, he'd acquired multiple startups, including an e-commerce company that was giving Amazon a run for their money.

The man was filthy rich and too powerful for his own good.

Katie had followed a story lead and had broken into his office building. She'd been caught and arrested. Then she'd been denounced by her network, fired, and publicly scolded by Donovan for her actions.

She hadn't spoken about what happened or why she'd been in his office, but most of the public simply assumed she was digging for dirt on the man.

It seemed like the career she'd worked so hard to build had come crashing down in one fell swoop.

Katie cleared her throat as they pulled up to her car in the university parking lot. "This is me."

"So it is." Dylan didn't tell her that he'd followed her the night before and recognized her vehicle.

Before Katie got out of the SUV, she turned toward him. "I don't suppose I can talk you out of following me home?"

He shook his head, trying to look regretful—though he wasn't. "I'm a man of my word. If I told your father I would follow you home, then I will."

She pressed her lips together before nodding with resignation. "That's what I figured. I'll be watching to see if you can keep up."

He grinned. "Challenge accepted."

DYLAN STARED out the windshield as he headed down the road.

He didn't like where this case was going. The hits kept coming, proving the person behind these acts was relentless. However, the perpetrator didn't necessarily show a lot of thought or planning.

Did that mean that the person behind this wasn't a professional? Was he someone given to whims?

If Dylan had to guess, that seemed to be the case.

He followed behind Katie just as he had promised. When Katie parked in her driveway, Dylan pulled up behind her, put his SUV in Park, and climbed out to meet her on the sidewalk near her front door.

Katie waited for him there, gripping her purse on

her shoulder. "Duty fulfilled. Again, I'm sorry to trouble you."

"My duty isn't quite fulfilled. I did promise your father I would make sure you got inside safely." He nodded toward her front door.

Katie's eyes widened and, for a moment, she looked as if she wanted to object. Then she let out a sigh. "Why not? You've come this far, and I've already had to swallow my pride. A little more won't hurt."

She grabbed her keys from her purse as she walked to the porch and opened her door. With a sweeping motion, she extended her hand to invite him inside.

At least, *that* had been easy.

Dylan stepped inside and glanced around. Just as he'd expected, the house was neat and clean. The furniture featured simple lines, neutral tones graced the walls, and greenery seemed to add another layer of life to the place. Add to that a scattering of natural wood accents and the smell of citrus and sage, and the place fit her.

Dylan checked all the rooms before returning to the kitchen.

"Everything looks clear," he announced.

Katie leaned against the kitchen counter with her arms crossed. "Thank you. I really do appreciate it."

"Of course. It was no problem." He started toward the front door when Katie called his name. He looked back up at her.

A small wrinkle formed between her eyes, and her lips looked tight, uncertain. "Listen, since you're already here . . . why don't you just sit down a minute and have some coffee? I have some leftover cheesecake we could have since we didn't get dessert tonight."

Dylan stared at her a moment, surprised she'd made the offer. But he wasn't complaining.

"That sounds nice," he said instead.

Katie stared at him a moment before a startled smile spread across her face. "Perfect. Why don't you have a seat on the couch, and I'll get it ready for us?"

"That sounds great." The more time Dylan could spend with her, the better.

But he was starting to like her company entirely more than he should.

———

Katie hadn't intended on inviting Dylan to stay. But the offer had seemed natural.

Besides, he'd been somewhat of a lifesaver for her. Not once but twice.

Coffee and cheesecake seemed the least she could do to show her gratitude.

Katie came back into the living room a few minutes later with a tray lined with two cups of coffee and dessert. She lowered herself into the chair adjacent to him.

Why did she feel nervous? She'd interviewed dignitaries. Politicians. Actors and actresses.

Yet her assistant made her feel jittery.

It didn't really make much sense.

She cleared her throat, deciding to keep this conversation professional—that was her usual comfort zone and fallback. "I'm afraid someone might be targeting my father."

She knew someone was clearly targeting her. But because her father had been a senator, he'd had a bull's eye on his back one too many times. Had tonight's incident been aimed at her? Or her dad?

Katie still thought it was probably her, considering all that had happened recently. But redirecting the situation toward her dad might help distract Dylan so he didn't ask too many questions.

Dylan took off his glasses and set them on the table. "I suppose he's made enemies over the years also?"

"To say the least. You know what they say about politicians . . . everyone hates them."

He let out a chuckle. "I'm not sure that's what I've heard."

"That's the subtext of it all. Believe me."

"I'm sorry. It probably wasn't easy growing up in the limelight like that."

Katie shrugged and took a sip of her coffee. "I don't know. It wasn't that bad. I suppose it was good training for when I became a journalist."

Dylan leaned forward. "I meant it when I said that I used to enjoy watching you on TV. Your work is very impressive."

Her gaze fluttered down. "I didn't break into that office just to dig up dirt. I went into Donovan's office because I had a lead I couldn't ignore."

"I'm sure you had your reasons. You don't have to explain." He took a sip of his coffee.

"Call me crazy, but I want to. I know people think I was just being aggressive and trying to get ahead. But the truth is I discovered information that made it seem like Donovan is involved in a human trafficking scheme."

"What?" Dylan narrowed his eyes as he listened intently.

Katie nodded. "I just needed some evidence to prove I was correct. But Donovan caught on to what I was looking for in his office. He knew what I suspected. He threatened me. Said if I told anyone about my theories that he would ruin me—and my father. I wanted to go on record and tell people the truth. But I couldn't. Not without proof."

"Do you think that's what this is about? Are you still looking into him?"

"I am, but I'm being very careful. There's no way he could know this time around."

Dylan tilted his head in doubt. "I wouldn't be so sure about that. From what I've heard about Donovan, he has people everywhere."

"He's not the only person I've been looking into . . ."

Before Katie could finish that statement, her phone rang. She almost ignored it. But when she glanced at the screen, she saw Connie's name.

Tension immediately stretched through Katie's muscles, and she rose.

"Excuse me a moment." She paced into the kitchen and put the phone to her ear. "Hey, girl. What's going on?"

Her cousin's frantic voice filled the other line. "I'm in trouble. I need your help. There's no one else I can call."

DYLAN HEARD the apprehension in Katie's voice, and he stood also. He knew he'd have to play this carefully. But he desperately wanted to know what was wrong.

Katie lowered the phone as he approached, and her gaze met his. "I hate to call this a night, but my cousin needs to . . . to talk to me."

He knew there was more to that phone call than that. "Just talk?"

Katie shrugged, her stiff neck showing her hesitancy to share. "She's having some . . . some personal issues."

"You said you were going to talk to her. Are you meeting her somewhere or staying here?"

A flash of defiance filled her gaze. "It doesn't matter."

"Actually, after everything that's happened, I'd say that it does matter." Dylan stepped closer, wishing he had more time to earn her trust. "Why don't you let me help you, Katie?"

She stared up at him, and he saw the questions in her gaze. Why would she let someone serving as her assistant help her in her personal life?

But not all hope was lost. A flicker of interest lingered in her gaze as well.

"I don't have time to stand here and argue with you. Besides, my father would kill me if he knew I went out by myself after what happened earlier. You can come—as long as you understand that *I'm* in charge."

Dylan raised his hands, relieved that she'd said yes. "Of course. Why don't you let me drive?"

She grabbed her sweater and purse before nodding. "It's a deal. But I don't have any time to waste. Let's go."

Dylan pulled his keys from his pocket and stepped outside into the moderate spring evening. As usual, he scanned everything around him to make sure there were no signs of danger.

He saw nothing.

Only Maddox sitting in the SUV across the street.

He pretended like he didn't see anyone in the

SUV, unwilling to draw any unwanted attention to his colleague.

Instead, Dylan escorted Katie to his car, climbed inside, and headed out of the neighborhood.

"Where are we going?" he asked.

"I'll give you directions. But for now, head toward Asheville."

His eyebrows shot up. Even though they were on the north side of Charlotte, Asheville had to be at least two hours away.

But Dylan knew better than to ask too many questions right now. If he did, Katie would most likely shut down, and he didn't want that to happen. It wasn't too late for her to change her mind about having his help.

Instead, he remained quiet and waited as she gave directions.

But he wondered what exactly was happening here and how it tied in with the attempts on her life.

————

Katie's mind continued to race. She'd told Connie to stay out of this. Why couldn't her cousin have listened? Now she was in trouble.

Apparently, Connie had stayed late at work and had seen Kingston Baylor leaving with boxes from the warehouse. She'd followed him, only to notice a sedan behind her following her instead. It wasn't Kingston—but it could very well be one of his lackeys.

Connie had tried to lose the tail, but in the process, she'd run out of gas.

She'd fled from her vehicle and hidden in an old barbershop.

Then she'd called Katie for help instead of the police.

Katie wondered about the wisdom of that decision, but Connie didn't seem ready to pull the cops into this yet. Not until she had solid evidence, which Katie completely understood.

Now it was a race to get to Connie before these guys found her. Considering how far away Katie and Dylan were, it didn't look good.

Anxiety raced through Katie at that thought.

She couldn't let anything happen to her cousin. Connie was practically like a sister to her. A little sister. The little sister who had always wanted to follow in her footsteps.

But Katie had encouraged Connie to take a different path—not because she didn't think her cousin was capable. Katie knew the kinds of situations she'd gotten herself in the middle of. Unsafe settings. More than once, Katie had seen her life flash before her eyes.

She didn't want that kind of life for her sweet cousin. Connie was too kind. Slightly naive even, for that matter. She lived with an amazing sense of joy, and Katie didn't ever want to see that taken away from her.

Katie stared out the window at the dark nighttime sky on the other side. She was thankful Dylan hadn't asked too many questions. She didn't want to refuse to answer, but she had no other choice.

He was practically a stranger. There was no way she could trust him with this information.

"Where now?" Dylan broke the silence as they got closer to Asheville.

Katie glanced at the app on her phone—one that allowed her to see Connie's location. Both of them had added it to their phones, just for safety reasons. But this was the first time Katie had to use it to find Connie.

She rattled off more directions.

A few minutes later, they pulled into a rundown area on the outskirts of Asheville.

Katie checked her phone again and frowned. This was definitely where Connie had said she'd gone. But Katie hated to think about her cousin being out here alone right now.

It was so dark. The buildings looked so dilapidated. In the distance, three men lingered on the corner, looking like trouble as they exchanged something in their hands.

She pointed to the building. "Up there. That's where Connie said she is. Connie . . . that's my cousin's name."

Dylan's eyebrows rose. She knew what he was thinking. This was no place for someone to be by themselves, especially at this time of night.

Katie didn't want to admit it, but she felt better having someone Dylan's size with her. His height and broad build would make someone think twice about approaching them—even if he did give off a bookish vibe.

He pulled to a stop by the curb, parked, and they hopped out.

A tremble raked through Katie, but she shoved those feelings aside.

Right now, she needed to think about Connie.

CHAPTER
ELEVEN

DYLAN FISTED his hands at his side.

He didn't like this. This area of town didn't seem safe.

He still had no idea what Katie's cousin might be doing out here at this hour. He'd prefer Katie not be out here with him looking for Connie. But he knew there was no way to talk her out of it.

He had a gun tucked into the holster beneath his jacket. Katie couldn't know it was there, but Dylan felt safer having it on him, just in case.

Katie walked beside him as they hurried toward an old barbershop. In the distance, the three guys on the corner glanced over at them.

No doubt they were assessing him and Katie as possible threats. Dylan had seen that look plenty of times, and he could read it from anywhere.

He hoped those guys didn't start trouble.

No one else was in sight, but that didn't mean they were alone. He wanted to ask Katie more questions, but he held himself back. He didn't want to scare her off or blow his cover.

Katie reached Erol's Barbershop and tugged on the door.

It was locked.

She looked around as if considering finding a brick or stone and breaking the glass.

Before she could, he nodded toward the large, broken window at the front of the building. "Let's go through here."

"Good idea."

He stepped inside first, tested the area, and then offered his hand to Katie. After a moment of hesitation, her fingers grasped Dylan's as she stepped over the broken glass and climbed inside.

Dylan had to admit that there was something about holding her hand that he liked. He hadn't had that reaction toward a woman since Rachel died.

He let go, not sure what to think about those thoughts or feelings. Besides, this wasn't the time.

"Connie?" Katie called as she stepped deeper into the dank space.

Litter and trash filled the old, abandoned shop. Six rickety barber chairs faced various directions around the room, and the checkout counter stood to their left. The mirrors that had once lined the walls were now cracked and missing large pieces.

A door stretched open at the back of the space.

From what Dylan saw, Connie was gone.

He pulled up the flashlight on his phone and shone it around. Katie started toward the back door, but he grabbed her arm and pulled her back. He'd rather be the first one through, just in case.

She opened her mouth as if to argue but then shut it again. Instead, she remained close to him, nearly glued to his shoulder as they moved forward.

Dylan stepped through the back door into the supply area. He shone his light around again, looking for any signs of life or movement.

Before he could call out for Connie, the stack of boxes to his right tumbled into him.

That's when he knew that they weren't alone.

———

Katie gasped as the boxes toppled into them.

Dylan pushed her out of the way before any hit her.

She scrambled to her feet, ready to retreat.

Then a familiar face caught her eye. "Connie?"

Her cousin's eyes widened. The next instant,

Connie was in her arms. The petite blonde cried on her shoulder, almost childlike in both stature and life experience.

"I thought I heard you, but I wasn't sure." Connie sniffled. "I was afraid those men had found me. I'm so sorry."

Katie held her cousin close. As she did, she glanced at Dylan to make sure he was okay.

He brushed dust off his shoulders before stepping back, unharmed.

But Katie noticed how he continued to scan everything around them.

Katie had observed that about him. He always seemed alert and on guard as if expecting trouble. Part of her thought it was strange. Then she remembered his military background. Maybe those qualities had simply been drilled into him through his years of service.

She stored that possibility in the back of her mind, vowing to think about it more later.

Katie turned back to Connie. "Are you okay?"

Her cousin cried into her shoulder again before nodding. "I guess so. I was just so scared. I thought for sure those people were going to find me."

"We have a lot to talk about," Katie murmured.

Connie's gaze drifted behind her to Dylan.

"This is my . . . my friend, Dylan," Katie said. It

didn't seem right to call him her assistant right now. "He's a good guy. You can trust him. I wouldn't have brought him otherwise. Dylan, this is my cousin, Connie."

They both nodded to each other.

Katie glanced around, still anxious that someone might have followed them inside. "Let's get you out of here before we run into any more trouble."

Connie didn't argue as Katie led her back toward the entrance. Dylan stepped through the window before helping them outside. Then Katie scanned the streets as they walked toward his SUV.

The three guys still stood on the corner. Still watched them. But they hadn't started any trouble. Not yet.

Instead of climbing into the front seat with Dylan, Katie sat in the back with Connie, knowing her cousin would need support.

Then Dylan took off down the road.

CHAPTER
TWELVE

DYLAN'S MIND raced as he headed back toward Charlotte as Katie had instructed. The two women sat in the back seat, Connie crying on Katie's shoulder as the two of them whispered.

Maybe he shouldn't, but he tried to listen and pick up on any clues about what happened. While he wanted to give the two of them privacy, he also needed to know details in order to keep Katie safe.

The whole situation was complicated, to say the least.

From what he picked up on, Connie had been following someone, only to have the tables turned on her. After running out of gas, she'd fled and hid.

What Dylan wasn't clear about was who had followed her, why, and if this was somehow related to the recent threats against Katie.

"We should go back to my house." Katie's decisive voice cut through the silence.

"Are you sure that's a good idea?" Dylan glanced in the rearview mirror and saw Katie jerk her eyes up to meet his gaze.

"Why do you ask that?" Suspicion laced her voice.

He swallowed hard before pleading his case. "I don't know what's going on here, and I don't want to pressure you guys to tell me anything you're not comfortable saying. But from what I've picked up on, someone knows Connie saw something she shouldn't. So now they're going to try to find her."

"Keep going."

"One of the first places this person will look is with any of Connie's family or friends," Dylan said. "Judging by how close you two appear, pictures of the two of you together are probably plastered all over social media. That means these guys will most likely check out Katie's place."

Katie stared at him.

He shrugged. "My best friend was a cop. He taught me a thing or two."

He expected Katie to question him, but she didn't.

"What do you suggest?" Katie asked instead. "We can't spend the night in this SUV. I guess we could get a hotel."

He swallowed hard again. "I don't know how you're going to like this idea. You're welcome to get a hotel, but that doesn't seem safe either." Dylan tried to watch what he said and make sure he didn't sound like too much of an expert. "My apartment is on the outskirts of town. Three bedrooms in a gated complex. You're welcome to stay there. You can each have your own room. Then we can recalculate tomorrow."

"We?" Katie asked.

Dylan shrugged, trying to remain casual. "It looks like I'm involved at this point."

"I never meant to pull you into this."

"It's okay." His voice sounded reassuring, even to his own ears. "I just don't want to see you guys get hurt."

Katie remained silent a moment before she nodded. "Okay. If you're really okay with that, then maybe we should stay at your place—but only until we can figure out something else."

Relief filled Dylan. That had been easier than he had anticipated. But he was so glad that she'd said yes.

It would be much easier to keep them safe if he was close.

———

Katie's mind raced. She should have probably said no. Should have insisted on a hotel.

But the thought of her and Connie staying in some rinky-dink hotel room by themselves made a shiver race through her.

Although Katie didn't know Dylan well and it seemed inappropriate to stay at her assistant's apartment, it was a good idea. No one would guess she'd be with Dylan. Most likely, if someone had been after Connie, they wouldn't think to look at Dylan's place for her either.

It would buy them some time until she could figure out how to keep her cousin safe.

Maybe they should have called the police this evening. But if they did, then Connie would have to explain her theories. She had no evidence to back up her claims and making accusations like that would definitely get her fired. Plus, there was already a big enough target on her back.

Katie had seen firsthand what men in powerful positions could do with their clout.

They could ruin you.

She'd been through that herself and didn't want to see it happen to her cousin.

Twenty minutes later, they pulled up to a gated apartment complex on the edge of town.

Katie raised her eyebrows as she glanced at it. The

place was nicer than she'd anticipated. She didn't really know where she thought someone like Dylan would live. Maybe in a little bungalow similar to hers. A private place where he could work with his hands and enjoy some quiet while he read classic literature.

He seemed like the kind of guy who was okay being by himself and enjoying a simple life.

They drove through the gates before pulling to a stop in front of one of the buildings at the complex.

Dylan climbed out and looked around again before motioning for them to follow.

They climbed the steps to the third floor, and Dylan ushered them inside his apartment before clicking three locks in place behind him.

"It's not much, but hopefully it will work for a night," he said. "Let me show you guys to the spare bedrooms."

He led them down the hallway and opened one of the doors.

"We can both stay in here," Katie said. "We've been having sleepovers together since I was eight."

Dylan nodded. "Very well. As long as you're comfortable. I'll leave some towels and washcloths outside the door—maybe some sweatpants and T-shirts also. You have your own bathroom, but it's down the hall."

They stepped inside the spare bedroom, and Katie was grateful for a moment to regroup.

But Connie looked exhausted, with her pale complexion and heavy expression. Her arms trembled and her hair sprang from her ponytail in uncountable directions.

Katie turned to her cousin, worry coursing through her. "Why don't you take a shower and see if that makes you feel better?"

Connie nodded. "That does seem like a good idea."

As soon as Connie slipped into the bathroom and closed the door, Katie stepped from the room and found Dylan fixing a glass of water for himself in the kitchen.

She didn't like to share very many details about her investigations with other people. In the past, it had never worked out well when she did. She'd learned the hard way that other ambitious reporters wouldn't hesitate to steal her ideas so they could get credit.

Katie would never make that mistake again.

She needed to restore her reputation as a reporter. This story would help her accomplish that. Still, trusting others wasn't something that came easily to her.

Yet Dylan had risked a lot for them tonight, and he deserved at least to know *something*.

She paused near the kitchen counter and crossed her arms. "Do you have a minute?"

He nodded. "I do. Would you like some water?"

As soon as he asked the question, Katie realized just how dry her throat was. "Yes, that would be nice."

Apprehension thrummed inside her as she anticipated how much she should tell him.

And as she imagined how Dylan might receive any information she shared.

She prayed she was making the right choice.

CHAPTER
THIRTEEN

DYLAN SAT on the couch and waited for Katie to begin, knowing better than to rush her, even if he was anxious for answers.

"Thank you for everything you did tonight." Katie stared at the untouched glass of water in her hands. "I know you probably have a lot of questions."

He remained silent, waiting for her to continue at her own pace.

"My cousin thinks someone at the beauty supply company she works for has been stealing bottles of caustic products, and she's afraid they're planning to do something dangerous with them."

His eyebrows shot up. So that's what this was about?

It hadn't been what he'd expected.

"Caustic products . . . are used to make bombs."

Katie nodded and pulled her gaze up to meet his. "Exactly. That's what worries me."

"Have you ever thought about reporting this to the FBI?"

"I have. But it's complicated. There's no evidence, and I keep telling Connie she's not the one who needs to try to find proof of any crimes. I don't want her to put herself in that position."

"That's probably a good idea."

Katie glanced back at the bathroom door as if checking to make sure it was still closed. "However, Connie doesn't have a lot of common sense, if you know what I mean. I love her, but she's the last person who needs to be in this kind of situation."

Dylan's spine stiffened. "I'm glad she got away. That could have had a much different ending."

Katie took a sip of her water before nodding. "I know. I'm trying to figure out how to help her. Clearly, if someone is trying to obtain supplies to build bombs, I need to figure out a way to stop them."

"Or you need to let *the FBI* find a way to stop them." He kept his words gentle.

"Are they just going to take us at our word? As soon as the investigation gets going, Connie will be fired—or worse. It will be clear who blew the whistle. And I know what you're thinking. I'm not keeping this information from them so I can break a big story. But it's hard to know who to trust and how to handle these situations."

He nodded slowly. "I understand where you're coming from, but I still believe the feds would be the best choice right now. Connie can find a new job."

Katie pressed her lips together in a tight line. "I'm afraid these people are willing to kill rather than let her report them."

Dylan's jaw tightened. He could see where Katie's words might be true. But there still had to be a better way to handle this than taking matters into their own hands.

"Do you think that's why someone is trying to kill you? Maybe there's a connection."

Katie ran her finger along the rim of her glass as if deep in thought. "I wish I could tell you. But I don't know."

"But you've been looking into the company, haven't you?" If Dylan was reading Katie correctly, she was the driven type who loved justice. The last thing she wanted was for these guys to get away with something—especially if that something hurt others.

Her gaze shifted up to meet his. Not because she

was shy, Dylan realized. But because she was hesitant about who to trust.

"I've been doing some research, but I've been careful. I'm trying to see what I can uncover about Baylor Beauty. I've covered my tracks, though. I don't know how these guys would know what I've been doing."

"If it's not because of Baylor, then who is it? Donovan Sullivan?" He remembered their earlier conversation.

Katie shrugged. "That's what I'm trying to figure out. Unfortunately, I've made a lot of people angry with the stories I've reported. But also my family has always been a target because of my dad's political leanings and commentary."

"I'm sorry to hear that." Dylan's instinct was to offer her advice. But he had to be careful how he worded things, or she might become wise to who he really was.

"Thank you for listening." She stood, water glass in hand. "I'm sorry I pulled you into the middle of this, and I promise to get out of your hair as soon as I can. Tomorrow, for that matter."

Dylan rose as well. "Katie, you're not in my hair. I want to do whatever I can to help. I don't mind."

Her gaze remained unconvinced. "I realize that,

but it's not like you're trained for any of this. This is my mess, and I've got to figure out how to handle it."

"Just remember, there's nothing wrong with asking for help." His gaze met hers. "You can trust me, Katie."

But as he looked into her eyes, he saw a flash of fear.

She truly was afraid of trusting people, wasn't she?

Dylan needed to figure out how he could change that.

———

Katie's mind raced. She hadn't intended on sharing all that with Dylan.

In fact, sharing those details with him could put him in danger as well. That outcome wasn't what she wanted.

She'd meant it when she'd told him this was her mess and that she needed to figure out how to get out of it.

But what if Dylan was right? What if asking for help wasn't a bad thing after all?

The questions collided in her head.

She only wished she knew the best answer.

When she got back to the bedroom, Connie was drying her hair.

As Katie grabbed one of the T-shirts Dylan had left for them, she held it to her nose.

The scent of sandalwood filled her nostrils, and she relished the aroma a moment.

It was nice. Very nice. And the scent fit Dylan.

As Katie changed, she glanced at Connie, who stood at the dresser.

Katie was so glad her cousin was okay.

But how would she keep Connie safe? Should Katie talk to the FBI as Dylan had suggested? Could she trust them?

Those were all things she needed to figure out.

Several minutes later, as Katie's head hit the pillow, Dylan's image remained in her mind.

Katie was starting to like her assistant entirely more than she should. She had no right to be attracted to the man. University policy probably forbade her from dating a colleague anyway.

Not that she wanted to date Dylan.

But the man was handsome, kind, and strong. Yet he wasn't pushy. He didn't impose his own views on her and expect her to cave to what he wanted.

Katie's driving need for justice had put her in perilous situations more than once. But she was entirely too strong-willed to hand over control to someone else. In her experience, she'd found most dynamic men liked to be in control, to have things their way.

Maybe that was another reason why she'd never gotten married. Finding a man she was both attracted to and who accepted her for who she was felt nearly impossible. Most men expected her to dim her personality in order to let them shine.

"He's cute."

Katie snapped from her thoughts as she turned toward her cousin. She pressed the side of her face into her pillow before asking, "Who's cute?"

Connie's eyes sparkled as she brushed her hair. "Dylan. You like him, don't you?"

Katie shook her head and let out an impish laugh. "I don't know what you're talking about."

"I haven't seen you look at someone like that for a long time. Maybe not ever."

"Even if I was attracted to him, the timing is awful. Not only does he work for me, but there's a lot going on right now."

Connie's smile faded. "I know. And it's all my fault, isn't it?"

"Of course not. You're simply being vigilant. If Kingston is doing something with these supplies, the authorities need to know."

Connie nodded and sniffled again.

"Let's get some sleep tonight," Katie said. "But in the morning, we're going to need to talk about some options. Because if these guys are coming after us, I'm afraid they may not stop until we're dead."

CHAPTER
FOURTEEN

DYLAN AWOKE EARLY to make breakfast. He wasn't sure what Katie or Connie ate so he decided to make a variety. Scrambled eggs cooked in one pan and bacon in the other. Bread was in the toaster, coffee had been brewed, and he even had some orange juice on hand.

After hearing the news Katie had shared with him last night, he'd hardly been able to sleep. His thoughts had turned over possibilities of how to handle the situation.

After Katie had gone to bed, Dylan called her father to give him the update. Mr. Logan had been even more adamant that Dylan keep Katie in his sights.

Dylan couldn't argue his point. Clearly, something dangerous was going on here.

But the situation was complicated, especially since he couldn't come clean to Katie about who he really was.

What would Rachel think of his deception?

She wouldn't approve. Yet she'd always been his biggest cheerleader, the one who'd given him the strength to face each new assignment.

He missed that encouragement and support.

His life hadn't been the same since he'd lost her.

Katie emerged from the hallway and pulled Dylan from his thoughts. She wore the same outfit as yesterday, but this morning her blouse was untucked and her black pants rumpled. He would probably need to stop and let her pick up some clothes sometime today.

Still, despite yesterday's clothes and the lack of makeup, she looked beautiful. With the less put together look, she seemed so much more approachable, like her guard was down.

"Good morning." He fought the rush of attraction he felt for her. The spark surprised him. He hadn't expected to feel anything like this again.

Not after Rachel. His wife had been his dream woman, and there would be nobody else like her.

Except maybe Dylan didn't need to find someone like her.

Maybe his heart should be open to someone

different. Someone who was also amazing—just in different ways.

He set those thoughts aside and raised a piece of sizzling bacon. "I hope you're hungry because I made breakfast."

She paused on the other side of the island and sat down. "My nose woke me up. I can't resist bacon."

Dylan smiled. "Are you sure that's what woke you?"

He glanced at her as he retrieved another piece of bacon from the griddle and set it on a paper towel.

She frowned and leaned her arms on the counter. "Actually, I had a hard time sleeping last night. But I'm guessing you can tell that by looking at me."

"No, you look as beautiful as always." He realized what he said and clamped his mouth shut. "I mean—"

She waved her hand and offered a graceful smile. "Don't explain. I know I look like a mess. Anyway, I take it you didn't sleep well either?"

He shook his head, grateful she hadn't made a big deal out of his words. "I have a lot on my mind."

"Connie and I will get out of your way today. I promise." She held up a hand as if pledging her words were true.

He handed her a cup of coffee. "You don't have to do that. I know this isn't my thing. It's your life. It's

Connie's life. But I meant it when I said I wanted to help in any way I could."

"Thank you." Katie pushed a lock of hair behind her ear and took a sip of her coffee. "I really do appreciate your offer. I need to figure out what I'm going to do. I'm not there yet."

"Of course." He picked up a plate. "Now, what can I get you?"

A few minutes later, bacon, eggs, and toast filled her plate. Coffee was in front of her, and the two of them sat at the dining room table.

"Should we wait for Connie?" he asked.

She shook her head. "She needs to rest. I don't think she's been sleeping well ever since she began suspecting something was happening at Baylor."

Concern filled his eyes. "Have you thought anymore about reaching out to the FBI?"

Katie frowned and shook her head. "I don't want to. Not yet. Not until I have evidence. I hate to admit it, but my trust in law enforcement isn't what it used to be, not after . . ."

She didn't have to finish.

Dylan knew exactly what she was referring to.

The incident that had gotten her fired.

He leaned closer. "What would it take for you to go to the authorities?"

She picked up a piece of bacon. "I need something

more definitive. I need absolute irrefutable proof of what they're doing."

"And how do you recommend getting that?"

Even though it was just the two of them, she leaned closer. "I have the name of the guy Connie thinks is behind this. I'd like to tail him. Take pictures. See what he's up to."

Tension spread across Dylan's chest. "That doesn't sound like a good idea. In fact, it sounds pretty dangerous. What if you're caught?"

"I suppose it could be dangerous. But I've been in situations like that before. Besides, what am I supposed to do? Sit idly by and wait for them to kill me or Connie?"

That was *exactly* what he wanted her to do—only he wouldn't let either of them get killed. He'd like to tuck them both away somewhere safe and handle this himself. He knew that wasn't a possibility. Not with someone like Katie Logan involved.

"It's like we talked about last night—you don't know for sure that these guys are the ones coming after you."

She frowned and lowered the slice of bacon she held. "You're right. I don't. But we do know that something's going on there."

His gaze locked with hers. "If you go, let me go with you. It's not smart to go on your own."

Katie stared at him a moment, and Dylan waited to hear what she'd say.

He prayed she would agree.

Otherwise, his job today would be very, very complicated.

———

Katie contemplated her answer as Dylan patiently waited.

She liked being a Lone Ranger and didn't want to get anyone else involved.

Because getting other people involved also meant possibly putting them in danger, and that wasn't something she wanted.

But she knew going alone was risky. That having someone to watch her back would be wise.

"I shouldn't leave Connie here alone," she finally said.

"I was thinking about that." Dylan shifted as if forming his words carefully. "Just hear me out before you jump to any conclusions, okay?"

Instantly, Katie's lungs tightened as she anticipated what he might say. "Okay . . ."

"I have a friend from the military who's now a P.I. He happens to be in town. I could have him come here to stay and keep an eye on Connie. That way you and I could go and see what we can find out."

Trust Connie with a stranger? It wasn't ideal. "Do you trust this guy?"

"I do. His name is Maddox, and he's one of the good ones. He won't let anything happen to Connie. We don't have to tell him any details about what's going on either. He'll be happy just to stay here."

Katie considered those options a moment. "I'm not sure what Connie will think about this."

"The important thing is that she's safe."

He was right. That was their first priority. Katie might have to operate outside her comfort zone in order to make that happen.

"I agree," Katie said. "That *is* the most important thing. If you don't mind, see if your friend is available, and if he can come over. I can pay him—"

Dylan held up a hand to halt her thoughts. "I'm not worried about payment."

"But I'd be happy to pay him for his time. It's only fair. Then, if you're truly game for it, I'll take you up on your offer to accompany me. But I just need you to know that you're doing this at your own risk. I have no idea what the outcome is going to be and—"

"I'm okay with that." Dylan sounded sincere,

convincing . . . like he wasn't the type who'd deceive her, which she greatly appreciated.

With one more glance at him, Katie nodded, decision made. "We should finish eating and then we can get ready and go."

CHAPTER
FIFTEEN

AN HOUR AND A HALF LATER, Maddox arrived at Dylan's apartment.

The man was tall, dark, and grumpy—at least, that's what people thought about him at first. After a bomb had nearly taken his leg off, he'd suffered PTSD. Eventually, he found his way of coping—by crocheting beanies.

Dylan noted that Katie seemed fascinated by him, like she wanted to dive in and do a story on the former sailor turned P.I.

Or like she wanted to grab her cousin and run far away.

She must have decided Maddox was okay because she left Connie with him so she and Dylan could investigate.

Before hitting the road, Dylan and Katie stopped

at Katie's house to grab some clothes. Katie donned some black jeans, a dark T-shirt, and a dark hoodie. She also grabbed a black baseball cap and tennis shoes.

Then they set out toward Asheville again.

As Dylan drove, Katie shared what she knew about Kingston.

"He's twenty-four years old and has had some minor scrapes with the law—one for burglary and one for drug use. But his parents are super rich. They own the company, and, by all appearances, it seems like they use their money to make his legal problems disappear."

"How many people does this company employ?" Dylan asked.

"Around six hundred."

His eyebrows flickered up. "It's bigger than I thought."

"Yes, it surprised me at first too."

"Is he sending products to a shell company? Is that what's happening?"

"According to Connie, Kingston has been staying late at work and sneaking out bottles of . . . something. She thinks it's acetone. No one really questions why he's there so late. So, Connie checked the inventory both before and after Kingston had wandered near the supplies. Some plastic bottles were missing after he'd been in the warehouse. He could have filled them with something."

"Do you have his address?" Dylan asked.

"I do." Katie glanced at her phone. "He doesn't live too much farther away."

"So, what's your plan when you get there?" Dylan tried to leave the ball in her court. He was supposed to be her assistant, after all, and he didn't want to cause her any alarm. He needed to act like more of a sidekick.

Katie stared outside at the blurring landscape a moment. "I think we should stay in the shadows. I don't want him to see me, just in case he knows who I am."

"So, we'll figure out if he's home, and then if he goes anywhere, we'll follow, correct?"

"That's it exactly."

Dylan nodded, glad they were on the same wavelength. "Sounds like a plan then. Let's hope that we discover something."

———

Katie took a sip of her coffee as she stared out the windshield at the house where Kingston Baylor lived. Considering the guy was only in his mid-twenties, the place was nice. She would guess three thousand square feet. All brick on a decent-sized lot.

Four cars were parked in his driveway. Yet, from what she understood, Kingston lived alone.

She could only imagine the shenanigans that might take place inside. Wild parties where the rich and entitled felt they could do anything and get away with it. Drugs. Prostitution. Gambling.

Of course, she had no proof any of that happened. But, in her experience, those things were normal for people like Kingston Baylor.

She and Dylan had been sitting across the street from Kingston's house for an hour. So far, there had been no movement. Katie hoped they hadn't taken this trip for no reason. But she'd known before she came that was a risk.

"For the record, I thought you got the wrong end of the deal when you were fired from Stone Media."

Dylan's voice broke Katie from her thoughts, and she flinched at his unexpected words.

"Thanks," she finally croaked out. "I'm either a hero or a villain, depending on who you ask."

She'd been praised by some for her brazenness, compared to a modern-day Bob Woodward. Others had thought she was a disgrace and should be canceled forever.

It was a good thing she didn't really care what

others thought of her—only those who were important to her.

"I *am* curious. I know that right now we think
these guys could be responsible for the attempts on
your life. But is there anyone else specifically you can
think of who might want to harm you or Connie?"

His question was interesting. For a split second,
Katie almost felt like she was talking to a cop. Maybe
it was simply Dylan's military background coming
into play.

She let out a long breath. "I don't know about
Connie, but for me there's Stiles Finnegan, I
suppose."

"Who is Stiles?"

"He's the needy student at the university who
came into the office probably three times yesterday to
ask various questions. You remember him?"

Dylan nodded slowly. "Yes, I remember him.
When you say he's needy . . . do you mean that as in
he's a little too interested in you?"

A frown tugged at her lips. "Possibly. I've been
trying to keep my distance from him just to be on the
safe side."

"Probably a good idea." Dylan's jaw tightened.
"Anyone else?"

"Every once in a while, I'll run into Donovan
Sullivan—or some guy that works for him—and that

always gives me pause." Just hearing Donovan's name caused her gut to cinch.

"Donovan Sullivan, huh?"

"That's right. Multi-millionaire. Business tycoon. A man who basically feels like he's untouchable."

Dylan shifted to face her, looking truly curious—or was it concerned?—about her statement. "And you sometimes just happen to run into him or his guys?"

Dylan was no dummy. Certainly, he had to realize that it wasn't a coincidence that she was back in Charlotte, the very place where Donovan's companies were headquartered.

She'd been in town visiting her father and had attended a function with him at a local museum. She'd been looking for a bathroom when she overheard a conversation between men about some "goods" they were transporting.

She'd stayed and listened, only to discover that Donovan was one of the men having that conversation.

She'd met the man a couple times before and didn't think highly of him. But his conversation made her curious. Maybe too curious.

That evening, she'd followed Donovan's right-hand man when he left the fundraiser. He'd gone inside a small office building belonging to one of Donovan's companies.

Katie had slipped in behind him. When he'd left his computer unattended, she'd jumped on it to see if she could find out more information. That's when she found pictures of foreign women, along with passports and visas and some kind of application.

She'd snapped some photos and left before anyone caught her. At home, she'd researched one of the women—Angel Tajan—going so far as to call her family in the Philippines. The woman's father told Katie that she'd come to the US to take a new job. But he hadn't been able to get in touch with her since she arrived, and he was worried.

A theory had begun to form in Katie's mind.

Had Donovan Sullivan moved from being a business tycoon to having some kind of involvement in human trafficking?

That's when she'd known she couldn't back off. One night, she'd hidden in a bathroom in Donovan's office building. She'd waited until everyone left, and then she'd snuck out. She'd gone into Donovan's office to search for more information—to search for proof of what he was doing.

But Marvin Pearsall, Donovan's right-hand man, had caught her and called the police.

Things had spiraled from there. After she'd been

fired, she'd decided to move to Charlotte to be closer to her father—and to Donovan Sullivan.

Whatever he was up to, she was going to get to the bottom of it.

"Katie?"

She glanced at Dylan, her thoughts returning to the present.

He'd asked her about "accidentally" running into Donovan or his men.

She remembered the feeling of being followed. Watched. The threatening texts and phone calls. The smirk Donovan gave her whenever they ran into each other.

"Donovan just wants to let me know he's still watching, and he wants to keep me in my place," Katie finally said. "He clearly realizes I'm suspicious about what's going on. Something else I noticed when I looked at his track record was that several people who've opposed him have mysteriously died."

"Really?" Dylan's voice lilted with surprise.

"Really. I still can't believe no one's been prose-cuted or that the FBI hasn't figured it out yet. But money talks. I hate to say it. For a long time, I was idealistic and thought most people were good down deep inside. But, lately, I'm not too sure."

She glanced at Dylan and saw surprise light his gaze.

She should regret her words. But she didn't.

They were true.

"I'm sure everything you've seen in your job can make you feel jaded," Dylan finally murmured.

"You can say that again. I just don't know why people have to lie. I suppose I pride myself on being blunt—and that's not always a good thing either. But I'll take bluntness any day over being deceived."

Most people who were deceptive had secrets—secrets that painted them in a negative light.

That was why Katie had worked so hard to uncover the evil acts people were hiding. One of her colleagues had pretended to be her friend only to stab her in the back. She still had trust issues to this day because of it.

No one deserved to get away with hurting other people.

No one.

DYLAN HATED that he couldn't tell Katie the truth. How would she react when she found out who he really was? Would she refuse to see him again?

What if he became another person on the list of people who'd disappointed Katie? Who made her jaded?

He licked his lips, wondering what it would be like if he told her the truth. If he got everything out in the open. If he explained the situation.

But he couldn't do that. Dylan had promised her father that much.

Still, it was bound to happen one way or another. Eventually Katie would find out.

Dylan knew when she did, everything would change.

Katie, against all odds, had begun to show trust in

him. The fact she'd allowed Dylan to come with her today spoke volumes. Dylan hated knowing that one day she'd resent this—that she'd resent *him*.

One day at a time, he reminded himself. That's what Rachel always told Dylan if he started thinking too much about the future instead of being in the present.

She'd been full of wisdom and grace. As a kindergarten teacher, her skills had come in handy.

Dylan's hand fisted again as he thought about how tragic her death had been. The person who'd ruthlessly killed her was now spending the rest of his life behind bars, which should bring Dylan comfort. However, once the drugs had left the killer's system, the man had been full of tears and regret.

Dylan knew he had to forgive the man. Maybe Dylan had in some ways. But other times, a swallow of emotions rose in him, and resentment took center stage.

He'd concluded that every day he had to make it a point to choose forgiveness. Unfortunately, it wasn't a one-step process for him.

Suddenly, Katie sat up straight in her seat. "There he is."

Dylan pulled himself from his thoughts and glanced up in time to see Kingston Baylor leaving his house with another man. Kingston had messy brown hair, was of medium height and weight, and dressed in baggy jeans and a blue T-shirt. A cigarette hung from his mouth, and he strutted as if he owned the world.

The two climbed inside a red truck before taking off down the road.

A few seconds later, Dylan eased out behind them.

"Don't get too close," Katie warned. "We don't want them to spot us."

Dylan wanted to tell her he'd done this hundreds of times before. But he didn't. Instead, he hung back farther as she instructed.

Kingston traveled through the outskirts of town and up into the wooded mountains. It would be harder to remain hidden on the narrow, winding roads. But Dylan would do his best.

Fifteen minutes later, Kingston turned onto a private gravel road that cut into the woods.

Dylan paused as the truck disappeared from sight. "There's no way I can follow him down that road. We'll be too obvious."

"What do you suggest we do?" Katie glanced up the drive.

Dylan let out a breath. What he wanted was to take Katie home, where she'd be safe. But he knew that wasn't an option right now. She was in this, with or without him.

"I'll find a spot on the side of the road where we can stash my SUV. Then we'll go the rest of the way on foot. But we're going to have to be very careful to make sure these guys don't see us."

Katie nodded, a new determination in her gaze as she stared into the distance. "Let's do it."

———

Katie stayed behind Dylan as he navigated a path through the thick, steep woods. She was thankful she'd dressed appropriately so she could stay hidden and navigate this terrain.

The path leading up the side of the mountain off the main road was longer than she'd anticipated. She and Dylan stayed a safe distance from the driveway in order not to be spotted.

It felt like they were never going to reach their destination.

"You ever met this Kingston guy before?" Dylan asked.

"No, never. Unless he somehow caught wind that I was looking into him, he shouldn't recognize me."

"Could he be the one behind the threats against you?"

Katie swallowed hard. "I've considered it. But, like I said, I've tried to cover my tracks. I can't see how he would have discovered what I'm doing."

"Maybe he suspects Connie knows something," Dylan suggested. "He could have looked into her background and discovered the two of you are related. Maybe he had one of his guys follow her."

"I suppose it's a possibility. But, at this point, I really don't know."

Finally, she spotted a clearing beyond the trees ahead. Indiscernible voices drifted with the breeze.

Dylan put his hand on Katie's back to indicate she should freeze.

She crept up beside him and ducked behind some bushes for a better view.

Kingston had parked in front of an old farmhouse and now unloaded clear plastic containers from the back of his truck.

Dylan grabbed his phone and snapped some pictures.

From this distance, it was nearly impossible to see exactly what was in those containers. They looked like gallon-sized bottles filled with a clear liquid.

Could the substance be acetone—or, even worse, triacetone triperoxide? The explosive substance was made from acetone and could be deadly . . . especially in these amounts.

"What is this place?" she whispered.

"Good question," Dylan muttered.

Not only was there the old farmhouse, but a couple of barns stood beyond that. Probably twelve vehicles were parked here altogether, and people—mostly men—moved around the property as if on a mission . . . though what kind Katie couldn't imagine.

Interesting.

Could this place simply be a fun getaway location for these guys?

Or was there something more sinister going on?

Katie and Dylan continued to watch.

She leaned forward, trying to get a better look or to hear a snippet of their conversation.

As she did, a crack sounded.

She froze.

Her knee had hit a stick.

She glanced up as panic tried to seize her.

One of the men closest to them glanced in their direction. "What was that?"

Katie held her breath as she waited.

"Probably just an animal," one of the men said.

Her heart thrummed in her ears as she waited to hear what they'd do.

"We should probably check it out, just to be sure."

No . . .

One of the men stepped their way, his gaze narrowed as if searching for trouble.

As he did, Dylan took her hand. "We need to get out of here. Follow me. And stay low."

He gently pulled her through the woods.

Katie prayed that they would get to where they needed to without being caught.

DYLAN KNEW it was a bad idea to bring Katie out here.

Now he had to make sure those guys didn't find them. They had to watch their every move. One more misstep could mean the difference between life and death.

Thankfully, Katie was nimble on her feet.

As they continued down the mountain, men yelled behind them, and feet pounded through the underbrush.

The faster he and Katie moved, the more noise they would make.

That would cause these guys to find them more easily.

On a whim, Dylan pulled Katie into a rocky

outcropping. He slipped behind some boulders and found a small, almost cave-like overhang there.

He pushed Katie deeper into the crevice and pressed in close to her.

She glanced up at him, her eyes wide with fear.

He felt her heart pounding against his chest.

But he mostly focused on the footsteps pounding their way.

"You sure you heard something?" one of the men said.

"Yeah, I'm sure. I think someone's out here."

"It was probably just an animal."

"We can't just let this go. We need to be certain."

Dylan held Katie in place, willing her not to make any sounds. Praying those guys didn't think to check this area.

If he had to guess, he'd say there were four men out there looking for them.

He glanced at Katie again and saw her eyes were closed. Was she praying also?

Dylan squeezed her bicep, trying to reassure her everything would be okay.

He had his gun and would use it if he had to.

But then his cover would *definitely* be blown.

As he waited, a footstep sounded probably only six feet away.

Dylan held his breath, and his hand went to his

gun beneath his jacket, but he didn't take it from the holster.

Not yet.

He would wait another moment first so he could be certain when it was time to act.

———

How could Dylan seem so calm at a time like this? Katie's heart raced out of control and sweat covered her forehead.

These guys were going to find them, and it would be all her fault. She should have stayed in place like Dylan had instructed.

She heard footsteps. Knew these guys were close. Knew they most likely had guns. Knew that she and Dylan could be goners.

And for what? They hadn't proved anything.

But knowing about this remote location did give her more insight. More opportunities to research.

If she survived.

Dylan pulled her deeper into the shadows, his body close to hers. She had to admit that being this close to him made her feel safe and protected. How could someone content to work at a desk seem this capable?

She wasn't sure.

But Dylan did seem proficient.

She continued to hold her breath as they waited.

"You're right," one of them finally said. "It must have been an animal. Let's get back before Kingston asks too many questions."

A few minutes later, the footsteps faded.

Katie and Dylan waited several minutes afterward just in case this was a trap.

Finally, Dylan's muscles softened just slightly, and he stepped back.

But not that far back.

He was still close enough to lean into her ear and for his breath to tickle her skin as he said, "We should get out of here. It's not safe to go back to that house right now. Not when they're so suspicious."

That was exactly what Katie was thinking too.

After she nodded in agreement, Dylan grabbed her hand again and began leading the way.

Normally, she would tell someone she didn't need them to hold her hand. But she justified it this time. Dylan was only trying to help them stick together.

Still, there was something about feeling his fingers intertwined with hers that made her feel connected and safe. She liked the feeling more than she would have thought.

Finally, they reached the SUV and climbed inside.

They'd made it back safely.

But Katie knew they weren't out of the woods yet . . . literally or figuratively.

CHAPTER
EIGHTEEN

AS DYLAN DROVE AWAY from the area, he glanced at Katie and carefully tried to formulate his words. "Do you think this is enough evidence to go to the FBI?"

Katie's jaw seemed to harden as she stared straight ahead. "I don't think so. We have to be sure of what was in those containers."

They were going to have to get closer if they wanted answers. But he wasn't about to say that to Katie. He knew that she would want to jump in and be right there on the front lines.

"I'm sorry you weren't able to get more answers." Dylan meant the words—on more than one level. He wanted a conclusion to this for her sake. So she could be safe. So those she was fighting to help would be rescued.

"Me too. I've got to figure out where to look next. Time isn't on my side right now."

"Are you ready to go back to my place?" Dylan almost dreaded hearing her answer. She wasn't one to give up—an admirable trait.

But not when he was trying to protect her.

"I'm not sure yet." Katie frowned, but her focused gaze made it clear she was deep in thought. "I don't know if I should keep following this Kingston guy, hoping to find some answers, or not. Maybe I should try to sneak back here after dark and—"

"That sounds like a terrible idea." That was *exactly* what Dylan feared Katie might say.

She swung her gaze toward him. "How else will I find answers?"

"Let's just keep thinking. There's no need to do anything rash."

Katie nodded as if considering his idea. But knowing Katie, once she got something stuck in her head, she went for it.

That was why Dylan needed to redirect her thoughts if possible. "We should probably check on Connie."

"That's a good idea." Katie's lips pressed together. "I want to make sure she's doing okay."

Dylan released his breath, thankful that Katie had accepted the change of subject.

Twenty minutes later, Katie ended her phone call and lowered her cell phone into her lap. The tension in her shoulders eased slightly.

"Connie said she's doing fine," Katie said. "She's been keeping busy catching up on some TV shows."

"That's good news, right?" Dylan glanced at her.

Katie couldn't begin to express how relieved she was to hear that update. "It's *very* good news. I don't know what's going on here, but I don't like my friends and family being in danger."

"That's understandable."

Dylan pointed to a small diner that appeared on the side of the road. "I'm feeling pretty famished. How about you?"

"Now that you mention it, I'm hungry also."

He pulled into the gravel parking lot, and the two of them walked up the wooden steps leading to the small building. A waitress in her fifties greeted them at the door, quickly looking them over.

Maybe stopping here hadn't been a good idea, Katie mused.

This seemed like the kind of place where everyone knew each other.

Everyone except them.

They were seated in a corner booth amid glances

of onlookers eating homestyle meals. The smell of collard greens, fresh pork barbecue, and onions drifted in the air.

Katie glanced over the laminated menu in her hands. "Anything look good to you?"

"I'm thinking about the Salisbury steak. I haven't had one of those in a long time."

"Not a bad choice if you're looking for some comfort food."

"Comfort food sounds really good about now." Dylan offered a quick, knowing smile. "How about you?"

"The chicken fried steak is calling my name." She set the menu down decisively.

"Also a good choice. That was always Rachel's favorite."

Katie's heart rate quickened at the mention of his wife. She shouldn't be so curious about the woman. Then again, she was a reporter. It should be expected, right?

Still, there was being curious and then there was prying . . . a thin line existed between the two.

She cleared her throat before softly asking, "If you don't mind me asking, how long were you married?"

"Five years."

"What happened?"

His gaze darkened, and Katie thought for sure he

would refuse to answer. But to her surprise, he rubbed his jaw before saying, "She was at a local park taking a walk when a man desperate for drug money shot her and took her purse."

Katie shook her head and held back a gasp. "I'm so sorry. For her death to be so senseless on top of your loss . . ."

He shrugged, though Katie saw the tension in his jaw.

"I was actually deployed to the Middle East when it happened. Rachel was in a coma in the hospital for three days. I tried to make it back in time but . . ." His voice cracked.

"I'm so sorry." She could only imagine how hard that must have been to be so far away during a tragedy like that. "Is that one of the reasons you got out?"

"It is. It took me a couple of years to solidify that decision. But I realized I wasn't really great at doing my job while dealing with grief. It was better if I got out. Besides, I'd put in my time."

"How did you and Rachel meet?"

The waitress came with their water and took their orders. As soon as she hurried to another table, Dylan turned back to Katie.

"Mutual friends introduced us," Dylan said. "It wasn't exactly a dramatic story or meetup. But the two of us hit it off right away. We were married six months after we first met."

"That sounds wonderful, actually."

"How about you?" His inquisitive eyes met hers. "Ever been married?"

"Not many guys can handle me." Katie decided to keep it simple. She shrugged, almost feeling apologetic as she said the words. "And I have very high standards."

He smiled, his blue eyes glimmering. "Nothing wrong with that."

As Katie stared across the table at him, she knew without a doubt her feelings for the man were beginning to grow—whether she wanted them to or not. She was *definitely* attracted to this man. Physically, emotionally, even intellectually.

It had been so long since Katie had felt this way that she didn't even know what to do about it.

So, she did what she did best.

She asked more questions.

"What are your dreams for the future?" she started. "Certainly, you don't want to work as an assistant in academia forever. Not that there's anything wrong with it if you do. Something about you working that job just doesn't gel with me, though. Not after the excitement of being in the military."

"I'm not really sure what I want." Dylan shrugged. "I'm still trying to figure it all out. I'm in a good place in my life where I don't have a lot of financial pressure, so I can take my time and figure out exactly what I want to do."

"I understand."

His answer was a lot different than hers would be. Katie had wanted to be a journalist ever since she could remember. Even now, chasing leads got her blood pumping.

Before she could ask any more questions, she heard the bell over the front door jangle, and she glanced up.

The air left her lungs when she saw Kingston Baylor step inside.

Had he followed them here?

CHAPTER
NINETEEN

DYLAN SAW Katie's eyes widen, and he glanced behind him.

Kingston Baylor had stepped inside the restaurant.

What was he doing here?

Quickly, he turned back to Katie. "Get down."

She didn't ask any questions. Instead, she sank low into the booth, bending toward her purse as if looking for something. She'd said she didn't think Kingston had seen her before, but they shouldn't take any chances—not if they didn't have to.

Kingston's back was toward the door, and Dylan and Katie were seated in the corner. With any luck, this guy wouldn't notice them.

Just as that thought raced through his mind,

Dylan heard footsteps and saw Kingston striding toward them.

Dylan's back muscles tightened as he braced himself for a possible confrontation. He prayed things didn't turn ugly. Especially not in here.

Not when considering there was a family with small children sitting two tables over.

"Don't I know you?" Kingston paused at the table, his eyes narrowed with suspicion.

Katie popped back up but kept her gaze averted. Dylan glanced at Kingston but didn't see any flashes of recognition in the man's eyes.

Dylan's heart pounded harder, but he was determined to stay calm. "Can't say I recognize you."

That was the truth. Before today, Dylan had never seen this man before. So, if Kingston recognized him that would be another mystery they needed to solve.

Kingston's gaze went to Katie, and Dylan froze. Dylan would pull his gun out if he had to. But the last thing he wanted to do was to draw a weapon in a restaurant with innocent civilians.

"And you." Kingston's eyes narrowed as he glanced at Katie. "I've definitely seen you before."

"I don't think so." Katie straightened, that stubborn, willful determination in her gaze.

Dylan silently pleaded with her to back down.

The last thing he wanted was for this conversation to turn ugly.

"What brings you to town?" Kingston turned back to Dylan.

"We were in Asheville for the day," Dylan answered. "But we decided to drive out to one of the waterfalls, and we saw this place on the way back."

Kingston stared at him another moment and let out a grunt.

Then his gaze turned back to Katie, and he observed her a moment. Katie refused to look away from the man or show any sign of weakness.

Part of Dylan admired her for that. But another part of him feared what might happen to her if she didn't back down.

"I've definitely seen you before," Kingston grumbled. "And I know where."

Dylan braced himself.

Was this the moment when everything would go south?

———

Katie waited to hear what he had to say. Waited for things to turn ugly.

"You were that news reporter, weren't you? For Stone Media?"

A smidgen of air left her lungs, and she nodded. "That's right. That was me. Katie Logan."

Kingston's eyes narrowed. "And you got fired for doing dirty investigative work."

"There was nothing dirty about it."

Dylan nudged her under the table. She knew she shouldn't bring any more attention to herself than necessary, but this guy was already getting under her skin.

"Don't get me wrong. I like a person with guts. I say, go for it. Anyway, I hope the two of you enjoy your visit to Asheville. It's a great place."

As soon as Kingston walked away from the table, Katie released her breath and glanced back at Dylan. His expression mirrored how she felt.

Relief.

All along, she'd wondered if Kingston could be behind the threats against her. She knew he could have caught on to the fact she was looking into him. But, based on the conversation they'd just had, that wasn't the case.

"I don't think he knows what I've been looking into," Katie whispered, unable to hide her surprise.

"If he doesn't, then he's not involved in the attempts on your life," Dylan said quietly. "And if that's the case, then who is?"

The question hung in the air.

Their food came, and they quickly began eating.

Katie couldn't wait to get out of this restaurant and away from Kingston.

DYLAN GLANCED at Katie in the seat beside him as they drove back to Charlotte.

Her eyes were closed, her head leaned back against the seat, and her chest rose and fell at a steady cadence.

She was sleeping.

A slight smile tugged at his lips.

Good. She needed some rest. He doubted she'd gotten much sleep over the last several nights.

Dylan was glad Katie felt safe enough to let down her guard when she was with him.

Still, his mind raced over everything that had happened.

Kingston hadn't seemed to recognize Katie as anyone other than a former news reporter. Did that mean they were chasing false leads in thinking he was connected to the threats surrounding her?

Dylan needed to look into some other suspects as well.

Donovan Sullivan seemed like a good option. Dylan would definitely be looking into the man as soon as he could. He had to pinpoint who was behind this if he wanted Katie to be safe.

Dylan enjoyed the quiet as he continued down the road. It wasn't until he pulled up to the security gate that Katie stirred. She blinked at Dylan several times as she sat up and looked around.

As he put his SUV in Park, she seemed to collapse back against her seat.

"I can't believe I fell asleep," she muttered, running a hand through her hair. "I hope I didn't snore. Or drool. Did I drool?"

He fought a smile and nodded toward her chin. "You just have a little bit right there."

Her eyes widened as her hand covered her lips and chin.

"Just kidding," he told her.

Katie playfully slapped his arm before rolling her eyes. "Oh, stop."

It was nice to see her relaxed. To seem a little less intense and determined.

However, Dylan knew the moment would be short-lived considering everything happening right now.

He climbed out and scanned the parking lot before escorting Katie to his apartment.

When they stepped inside, Dylan spotted Maddox and Connie playing Risk at the kitchen table.

Katie paused beside him and stared at her cousin, looking slightly perplexed. "You're wearing a . . . beanie?"

Connie grinned as she touched the teal hat. "Maddox made it for me. He makes them, sells them, and gives the profits to different military organizations."

Maddox shrugged and grunted as if it weren't a big deal.

That was Maddox for you. A man of few words.

"It looks . . . nice." Katie frowned as if she didn't know how to read Maddox.

The smile faded from Connie's face as she turned toward them, the lighthearted conversation seemingly forgotten. "So, what's the update? You can speak freely in front of Maddox. I've already told him what's going on."

Dylan and Katie exchanged a glance.

Then they dove into the details of today's adventures.

———

Katie purposefully waited until Maddox and Connie went to bed so she could have a moment alone with Dylan.

The two of them were seated on the couch. Dylan's arm stretched across the back but didn't quite reach her. For a moment, Katie wondered what it would feel like to lean into him. What it would be like to have his strong arms around her. To inhale his sandalwood scent.

She quickly shoved those thoughts aside and cleared her throat. "All I can think about is what's next."

Dylan shifted, his serious gaze making it clear all his attention was on her. "Maybe we should look at other possibilities as far as suspects. Maybe we should look into Donovan."

"Out of curiosity, let me see where in the world Donovan Sullivan is right now." Katie grabbed her phone.

"How are you going to do that?"

"By searching his social media." She typed something on her screen and then her eyes widened. "You'll never believe this."

"Try me."

"Donovan is opening a new business in Charlotte this week, and he's having a big soirée tomorrow night at his house."

"I wonder what the chances are that we could get in . . ." Dylan muttered, narrowing his eyes in thought.

Katie's lips twisted into a frown. "I know I won't be welcome. Most likely, by default, my father won't be welcome either."

Dylan leaned closer so he could see her phone. "What else does it say about the soirée?"

"It's for North Carolina business leaders."

Dylan sucked in a quick breath and rubbed his chin. "I might have an in for us."

Katie's eyebrows shot up. "Really?"

He really was a man of mystery—and he was one mystery she wanted to solve.

"Before I say anything, let me make some calls," Dylan said. "I won't share anything about what's going on with you. I promise. But I might be able to get us invitations."

Just as he said those words, Katie's phone buzzed. When she looked at the screen, she saw a new text message.

The words on the screen made her blood grow cold.

Mind your own business or next time I won't play so nice.

Someone was definitely watching her.
And her life was still in danger.

CHAPTER
TWENTY-ONE

THE NEXT MORNING, Dylan, Katie, Maddox, and Connie went to Katie's church.

Hearing that she attended every Sunday only made Dylan like her more. He'd always been a man of faith. Relying on God had gotten him through some of his darkest periods . . . like when he'd lost Rachel.

In some circumstances, Dylan wouldn't recommend leaving the apartment. But, with all that was happening, he knew he couldn't keep Katie in one place. That wasn't in her nature. Besides, he couldn't argue with church, especially not while claiming to trust God.

They'd swung by her house for her to change into some appropriate clothes—Katie had also let Connie borrow some—before heading out.

The church was on the larger side—probably close to a thousand, if he had to guess, and the building was modern. The lobby area smelled like coffee and pastries, and contemporary Christian music poured through tiny speakers mounted in the corners.

As they grabbed some coffee, Mr. Logan spotted them and strode over to greet them. "Great to see you all here."

"Good to be here," Dylan answered, exchanging a look with him.

Even though everyone seemed friendly, Dylan continually looked for any signs of trouble. He couldn't afford to let his guard down—not even in church.

As they headed into the auditorium to be seated, someone cut through the crowd toward Katie.

Dylan nudged himself in front of Katie as he prepared for a confrontation.

———

"Stiles . . ." Katie inadvertently moved farther behind Dylan, allowing him to protect her if need be.

It wasn't something she was accustomed to doing. She'd always been one to take care of herself.

Then again, she'd never realized how nice it felt to have someone watching her back.

Although her dad had always been there for her, this felt different.

In a good way.

"I didn't realize you attended Hope Community." Stiles' gaze wavered almost nervously.

"I could say the same for you."

"It's my first time. I've been checking out new churches in the area ever since I started at the university in the fall. I haven't found one I really liked yet." He glanced around, his shifty actions and gaze making his apprehension unmistakable.

"Well, I hope you'll like it here." Katie heard the slight tremble in her voice. She hated to be nervous. But after everything that had happened, how could she not be?

"I know I already said this, but I just want to let you know that I *really* think you're doing a fantastic job at the university," Stiles continued, sweat beading across his forehead. "I'm so glad you're there."

Katie forced a polite smile, still unsure about her student. But she would cautiously try to reserve any judgment. "I'm glad to be there. And I'm glad to have you here at church this morning. I think you'll find it very welcoming."

Something about the boy's appearance here made her a little uneasy.

When she first started out as a reporter at a local news station, a viewer had obsessively stalked her. Hank Kirkpatrick had sent her messages online. Messages to the station. Whenever he knew Katie was covering something, he'd shown up while she was on the scene.

Then one day, he'd come to her house.

After that, Katie had to file a restraining order.

Hank had finally left her alone. But Katie knew she was fortunate. That wasn't always the case.

She didn't want to relive that again.

Was the look in Stiles' eyes the same look that she'd seen in Hank's?

She wasn't sure.

As the church service got started, Katie had to do everything in her power to focus on the songs and sermon instead of the danger overshadowing her. The process seemed to define what it meant to bring the sacrifice of praise . . . because it took every ounce of her effort to redirect her thoughts.

CHAPTER
TWENTY-TWO

DYLAN DIDN'T LIKE everything that was going on. Didn't like the fact that Stiles was here.

Was his presence a coincidence?

Dylan had a hard time believing that it was.

All throughout the service he kept one eye on the preacher and one eye on Stiles, who sat on the other side of the auditorium.

He noticed how the college student would occasionally glance over at Katie. The guy definitely had some kind of crush on her. But was that where it stopped? Or had this crush turned into an obsession?

As soon as Dylan had a chance, he would look further into this Stiles guy.

When church was over and Dylan rose to leave, his phone buzzed.

It was a text from the contact he'd called earlier

about the soirée tonight. It appeared she'd be able to get Dylan and Katie into the event.

A sense of victory washed through him.

Immediately followed by dread.

While it was good news, he also knew it could be dangerous. Clearly, Donovan wouldn't welcome her at the party. That meant the two of them would have to keep low profiles in order to avoid being spotted and causing a scene.

That would be hard, considering the fact that Katie's face was so recognizable.

It also meant she'd need a dress and that Dylan would need a tux, which would create more situations that put them out in public and increased their chances of running into danger.

There was still a lot they needed to plan, and they didn't have much time.

Most of all, Dylan prayed he'd be able to keep Katie safe.

Especially when he remembered that text this morning.

Mind your own business.

He had too many unanswered questions right now.

As Katie talked to someone in the distance, Dylan glanced at Mr. Logan beside him.

Maybe this would be a good opportunity for the two of them to talk.

"Mr. Logan," Dylan lowered his voice. "I want to tell Katie who I really am. I don't like deceiving her."

Her father's gaze darkened. "She'll fire you."

"I think she'll understand."

"She won't."

"Then I'll protect her off the books. That way, maybe there won't be as many hard feelings at the end of this when she learns the truth."

Mr. Logan turned toward him. "It's either we deceive Katie or she could die. What do you pick?"

Dylan's heart lodged in his throat. He understood what Mr. Logan was saying. Katie would never accept help. If she learned the truth, she would push him away.

Then there would be more of a chance that the person targeting her would get what he wanted.

But just because Dylan understood didn't mean he liked any of this.

———

"You actually got us an invitation," Katie said as they climbed back into Dylan's SUV after church. Excitement raced through her at the possibility of what they might discover at this soirée.

Connie and Maddox climbed in the back seat and seemed lost in their own conversation about a movie they'd both recently seen.

That was good. It gave Katie and Dylan a chance to have some semi-privacy.

"I did manage to get us an invitation." Dylan pulled on his seatbelt. "We have only about five hours now to make sure we have something appropriate to wear."

"I'm sure we can manage that." She clicked her own seatbelt in place and stared out the window as her thoughts raced. "But if Donovan sees me there, he's going to recognize me."

"We'll keep a low profile."

She glanced at Dylan as they took off down the road, that certainty that he had secrets pressing on her again. There was more to Dylan Granger than met the eye.

"How did you get us in?" she asked.

"An old military friend of mine, Brandon Hale . . . he's dating the CEO of Embolden Tech. I seem to remember her saying once that she gets invitations to events like this one all the time, so I gave her a call. She and Brandon are going to meet us there."

His explanation seemed reasonable. "That's great news. Please thank your friend for me."

"I will." Dylan glanced at her. "But you're going

to have to be careful tonight." Worry stained his voice, almost as if he had second thoughts.

"Of course. I've learned to be careful." Besides, being caught was the last thing she wanted.

"I'm not sure exactly what we're going to be able to figure out by being there."

"I mostly just want to keep my eye on this guy and see if he seems to be up to something. See who he talks to. Maybe if he disappears into another room with someone."

Dylan nodded in resignation, almost as if he'd hoped she'd change her mind about going. "Of course. Let's grab some lunch, and then we need to go shopping."

"How about you take us back to your apartment?" Maddox turned to Connie. "Unless you want to go shopping too."

"I'm good with going back. I want to finish that game of Risk we started."

"That will work," Dylan stated.

Katie's mind raced as she tried to figure out where to look for a dress and how she could find out information while at the event.

BY THE TIME they finished shopping, Dylan and Katie had just enough time to eat, grab their clothes, and get ready.

Dylan gave one last glance at himself in his bedroom mirror and felt an invisible weight pressing on his chest.

The last time he'd worn one of these was for his wedding.

The happiest day of his life.

Why did it feel like another lifetime ago? Sometimes the pain felt fresh, like it was just yesterday. But right now . . .

He shrugged those thoughts off, knowing he needed to get moving. Emotions would only cripple him—something he couldn't afford while working this assignment.

He stepped into the living room and found Maddox crocheting on the couch. Dylan sat across from him, knowing he had some business to address before he left this evening.

"Were you able to look into Stiles?" Dylan started.

Maddox didn't miss a stitch as he answered. "As a matter of fact, I did. The guy has a clean record. Nothing on file as far as a criminal history. Nothing behavioral. He seems to be a pretty intelligent guy."

"But that doesn't mean he's not behind this." Dylan's lips flickered down in a frown.

"That's true. However, I cross-referenced some of the dates of the incidents—the shooting in particular. Turns out he has an alibi. He was at a debate club meeting that evening at the school. There are photos of him online, and I double-checked the times."

Dylan rubbed his jaw. "So, it looks like we can rule him out?"

Maddox shrugged as he finished a beanie and inspected it. "That's how it looks to me. I don't see how he could be responsible."

"Good to know."

Maddox glanced away from the knit hat in his hands. "Why do you look nervous?"

Nervous? Maddox wasn't reading him right.

"I'm anxious to see how things will go at this soirée tonight," Dylan answered. "I'm not sure exactly what we're going to find out, and I don't want to put Katie in another dangerous situation."

"I understand. You seem to be a little sweet on her." Maddox stole a glance at him.

"She's an amazing woman. I hate the fact that I have to deceive her."

"I get that. You're in a hard place."

He remembered his conversation with Mr. Logan earlier. "Even if I were to tell her the truth now . . . I'm still not sure she'd forgive me. She'd probably just fire me instead."

Maddox grunted. "You might be right. I wish I had some great advice to give you, but when it comes to social etiquette, you know I'm not your guy."

Dylan fought a smile. No, Maddox bucked social standards most of the time. It was part of what made him who he was.

"It's okay," Dylan said. "Thanks for listening."

Maddox slapped his arm. "In better news, you look like a million bucks."

Dylan glanced down at the black tux he'd rented. "Thanks. I appreciate that."

Before they could talk anymore, Katie stepped from the hallway.

As soon as Dylan saw her, he sucked in a breath.

She looked gorgeous in her navy-blue sleeveless gown. The dress was fitted at the top and flowed down to her ankles in silky waves. A pearl necklace graced her neck, and her hair, normally pulled back, fell over her shoulders in soft, feminine waves.

The less professional look nearly made her unrecognizable.

Connie slipped out of the room behind her, her face glowing with a smile as she looked at her cousin. "This is the Katie I remember from high school."

Her comment was curious. He wondered how Katie had become the person she was today. Maybe at some point she'd feel comfortable enough to share.

Katie cleared her throat as she glanced at her dress. "Do I look ridiculous? I always try to look professional and not too girly so people will take me seriously but—"

"You look beautiful," Dylan interrupted.

But another puzzle piece did fall into place. Katie hadn't become the reporter she was by seeing where life would take her. She'd planned each detail—even down to the way she presented herself. She was one determined woman.

Dylan couldn't be sure, but Katie may have blushed at his compliment. Her gaze fluttered to the skirt of her dress again. "Thank you. Are you ready to go?"

Dylan wasn't sure if he was ready to go or not,

but despite that he nodded. "Yes, we better get on our way so we're not late."

With a nod to Maddox and Connie, the two of them stepped through the door and headed toward Dylan's SUV. He placed a hand on Katie's back as he directed her across the parking lot.

Was it his imagination, or did she draw in a quick breath at his touch?

He didn't know.

But he did realize that there was something about the action that felt entirely too natural.

He prayed God would watch over them tonight. He'd already lost one woman in his life that he cared about. Though his feelings had only just started for Katie, he knew he didn't want to lose her also.

———

Katie stared at Donovan Sullivan's house as they pulled up in front of it.

It was even larger than she'd imagined. At least ten thousand square feet. Maybe more.

It was definitely what she'd call a trophy home. Big white columns, two wings spanning from the center, a large lot with lush green grass and a fountain out front.

Guests—arriving in luxury vehicles—pulled up to

the door, where a valet took the keys and parked for them. Men in tuxes and women in expensive, glittering gowns climbed the steps toward the front, where live music drifted out.

No expense had been spared.

"You ready for this?" Dylan asked as a valet pulled away in Dylan's SUV and they stood in front of the massive front doors.

"Am I ever." Katie slipped her arm through his as they followed the others inside.

The interior was just as impressive as the outside, with an expansive foyer filled with marble floors and tall ceilings and an ornate chandelier overhead. They were ushered into a space to their left—a large ballroom. No, it was a living room, she realized. Except all the furniture had been cleared to make room for this event.

Couples danced in the center of the room while servers offered champagne and hors d'oeuvres. The scent of pricey perfume lingered in the air.

Katie should be used to events like these. She'd attended uncountable ones with her father.

But she'd always felt out of place, no matter the circumstances.

Almost as soon as they'd stepped inside, a man and woman around Katie's age approached them. The man had dark hair and a muscular build, and the woman had blonde hair that had been pulled back in a twist.

Dylan's face lit up with a grin as he hugged them both.

Then he turned to her. "Katie, this is my friend Brandon and his lovely girlfriend, Finley. Brandon, Finley, this is Katie."

Katie grinned at the couple standing in front of her. "Thanks so much for the invitation."

"My pleasure," Finley said. "I'm a big fan of yours. Love your news stories and how you never back down."

"Thank you."

They made small talk for a few more minutes until Katie turned back to everyone around them.

What disturbed her the most was that some of these people might even know what Donovan was up to, yet they still supported him. Their reputation and social standing were more important than their ethics.

Or perhaps some of them were even in on it.

The thought burned her up inside.

It was just one more reason she wanted to take this guy down.

Katie would get answers concerning what Donovan was doing if it was the last thing that she did.

She glanced across the crowd, and she spotted the man at the back of the room talking with several members of the city council. He was stout, with a square face and ruddy complexion. In his sixties, he carried himself like royalty—and everyone around him treated him as such.

Her stomach turned when she watched him smile and laugh as he socialized.

It wasn't right that evil people seemed to live such easy, rewarded lives while others tried to do good and struggled. She knew that the only rewards Christians were promised here on Earth were things like peace in the midst of trials, that their true rewards would be in heaven.

Still, sometimes it just seemed wrong.

"Hey." Dylan touched her elbow. "Are you okay?"

She nodded, trying to keep her emotions in check. "I'm just fine. Thank you. I guess I'm feeling a little apprehensive."

"As would anyone in your shoes."

"I'll keep an eye on Donovan throughout the evening," Brandon said. "Just to make sure he doesn't get too close to you. There's something about the guy that I don't like."

"Same here." Katie didn't bother to hide the hardness in her voice. Her gaze stopped on someone across the room, and she sucked in a breath.

"What?" Dylan followed her line of sight.

"It's Kingston's parents. The Baylors. They're here."

"They are North Carolina business leaders."

She nodded, not taking her eyes off the couple. "They are. I guess I should have expected this almost. But . . . I don't know. I didn't."

She watched as the two mingled with all the guests.

She hadn't heard anything bad about the parents. Only Kingston. Still . . . she would need to keep her eyes open.

Dylan extended his hand toward her. "In the meantime, would you like to dance?"

The thought of dancing with Dylan brought a small thrill through her. "I would love to."

She placed her hand in his, and he pulled her toward the dance floor, putting his arms at her waist. She rested her hands at his shoulders, and they began swaying with the music. A five-piece band played Adele's "Make You Feel My Love."

If it weren't for the danger in this room, the moment would feel close to perfect.

She swallowed hard, her throat burning as she glanced up at Dylan. "I have to say you've really been a great sport about this. Not many people I know would go out of their way to do this for me. I just want to say thank you."

"You're welcome," Dylan crooned in that Louisiana accent she was beginning to love. "I'm glad I can be of help."

Dylan opened his mouth as if he wanted to say more but he clamped down again.

That feeling returned to her belly. The feeling that Dylan harbored some kind of secret.

He seemed like such an honest guy. What could he be hiding? Was it something she should be concerned about? Or was it something simple, like the fact that he wasn't over his wife's death yet?

Katie usually trusted her instincts, but in this case, her heart battled with her gut, and she wasn't sure exactly what to think.

Instead of overanalyzing it, she decided to enjoy the moment.

She leaned closer to Dylan and rested her head on his chest as they swayed to the music.

She loved feeling so close to him. Feeling the strong muscles on his chest. Smelling his sandalwood scent. Knowing that he was looking out for her.

How could someone who had considered herself such an independent woman be reacting like this? It didn't make sense. It defied logic. But it was true.

Maybe she just needed to tell Dylan how she was feeling. She'd always been direct. Why should anything change when it came to matters of the heart?

Before she could say anything, their gazes caught. Did Dylan feel the same thing she did? At the moment, she had no doubt he did.

As they paused on the dance floor, Dylan's hand cupped her cheek.

He was going to kiss her.

And she wasn't going to stop him.

Just as she closed her eyes and anticipated what it might feel like for his lips to touch hers, she heard someone step behind her.

"Good to have you here," a deep voice said.

Katie froze.

She knew right away who it was.

Donovan Sullivan.

CHAPTER
TWENTY-FOUR

DYLAN SHOULDN'T HAVE ALLOWED himself to be distracted. Because now Donovan Sullivan was right in front of them, and Dylan had to think quickly. From a distance, the man might not recognize Katie.

But face-to-face?

There was no doubt he'd know who she was.

Dylan grasped Katie's arms, keeping her facing him.

"Mr. Sullivan . . ." Dylan started. "This is a great party."

Donovan glanced at the back of Katie's head as if he expected her to turn around and introduce herself.

At just that moment, Brandon swooped in and extended his hand. "I'm sorry to interrupt, but it's my turn to dance. I've been waiting all night."

He took Katie's hand, and they glided across the dance floor away from Donovan.

Dylan released a breath.

That had been close.

"Who are you here with?" Donovan continued, his beady eyes appearing suspicious.

"Finley Cooper with Embolden Tech."

"Oh, yes . . . Finley." Donovan's voice seemed to perk. "She's a phenomenal woman. How do the two of you know each other?" He narrowed his gaze at Dylan.

This guy was *definitely* wary.

Dylan straightened the arms of his coat and plastered on a smile. "I'm actually friends with her boyfriend. We served in the military together."

"Military, huh? Well, thank you for your service." Donovan saluted.

"You're welcome."

With another quick scan of Dylan, Donovan moved on to the next guest.

Dylan released his breath.

That had been close.

A little *too* close for his comfort.

———

Katie watched as Donovan wandered to the other side of the room.

It was only then that her lungs loosened.

She glanced up at Brandon and nodded. "Thank you."

He paused on the dance floor. "It's no problem. He's a dangerous man."

Her gut twisted at his reminder. "I know."

"Be careful around him."

"I will." Just as she said the words, Dylan appeared beside them.

His gaze looked concerned as he observed her. "Mind if I cut in?"

"Not at all." Brandon stepped away.

As Dylan took her into his arms, her gaze locked on his. "What did Donovan say?"

"He was just asking questions. I don't think he's suspicious anymore."

She glanced over Dylan's shoulder, making sure Donovan wasn't coming back. "Maybe. It's hard to tell. I don't trust him at all."

Dylan twitched his head toward his shoulder. "Neither do I."

"Dylan, I want to go into his office here."

He stiffened under her touch. "That's a terrible idea. Why would you want to do that?"

"This might be my only chance to snoop around his personal effects."

He stared at her another moment. "What do you think you're going to find?"

"I have no idea. But there could be something there that offers a clue about what's going on. Dylan, I'm never going to have this opportunity again."

Dylan didn't seem to realize she wasn't asking permission. She was going to do this with or without his help.

He let out a soft sigh. "Do you even know where his office is located?"

"As a matter of fact, I read an article about him before we came. It had a picture of him in his home office."

"And . . ." Dylan waited for her to continue.

"The sun was setting behind him, and, based on the landscape on the outside of the window, the room was on the first level."

Dylan's eyebrows flicked up as if he was impressed. "That's observant. But still . . . this house is huge."

"My best guess is that it's on the west wing. That's probably where the bedrooms are."

"There are security guards stationed in that area to ensure no one wanders where they shouldn't."

She shrugged, still unfazed. "Security just needs a little distraction."

"Like what?"

She let out a soft breath. "I'm not sure. But I'll think of something."

CHAPTER
TWENTY-FIVE

DYLAN DIDN'T LIKE the sound of this. But he knew he couldn't stop Katie from searching Donovan's office.

She was determined to find out more information. So, Dylan could either help or he could pretend like he didn't know what was going on.

The second choice wasn't really an option.

He needed to pull Brandon into this, however.

"I'm going to run to the restroom," Katie told him. "Then, if I'm going to do this, I have to do it soon. This party will wrap up in a couple of hours. I don't have much time."

Tension embedded itself in Dylan's back muscles, but he ignored the tautness. Instead, he watched as Katie slipped into the bathroom. As he searched for

Brandon, he quickly reflected on the kiss that had almost happened.

What had he been thinking?

None of that had been planned—and it could have proved to be a huge mistake. He'd lost his focus, and Donovan had walked up on them.

Besides, he was on the job. Kissing clients was a major no-no.

He'd have to reprimand himself more later. Right now, he had a job to focus on.

Dylan found Brandon and told him what was going on.

"We have other trouble also," Brandon muttered.

He didn't like the sound of that. "What?"

"Joe is here."

"Joe Faulkner?" Dylan scanned the crowd around them until his gaze stopped on the man.

"The one and only."

Joe worked for a less-than-ethical security agency called Dagger. The man should have been arrested after an incident at Finley's company, but he wisely hadn't been onsite when the police had gotten involved.

Yet, now, here he was.

Was that a coincidence? Certainly, there wasn't some kind of tie between what happened at

Embolden—Finley's company—and what was going on with Donovan.

But what if there was?

Dylan swallowed hard.

Katie emerged from the bathroom, that same determined look still present in her gaze.

Dylan knew how this would go down.

She was going into that office.

And if she was caught . . . Donovan would make her life miserable.

———

Katie glanced around, searching for anyone suspicious, before leaning closer to Dylan and whispering, "If I'm going to Donovan's office, I need to head there now. There's no time to waste."

Donovan was still on the far side of the room, presenting this as the perfect opportunity.

Dylan's jaw flexed in disapproval. "How are you going to get past the security guard?"

Katie glanced at the man. He was probably in his fifties, with a robust belly and a gaze that continually went to the trays of food being served to the party guests.

He was hungry, she realized.

"I have an idea," she murmured to Dylan before slipping away.

A few minutes later, she walked back, one of the servers trailing behind her carrying a food tray.

As Katie veered off toward Dylan, the staff member stopped at the corner of the hallway and called the guard over.

"What did you do?" Dylan whispered.

"I paid her a few bucks to offer some food to the guard. I told her he was feeling lightheaded. Now, I've got to run."

While the guard was distracted, she slipped past. She quickly glanced behind her, making sure no one watched as she hurried down the hallway.

So far, the coast was clear.

She tried the first door.

Bedroom.

The next door was also a bedroom.

Finally, the third door . . . was locked.

Katie frowned. Of course, it was locked. She should have known.

But, at least, she was always prepared.

She reached into her purse and pulled out a lock-picking kit. She kept one on hand for occasions such as this. She'd only had to use it twice before, but she tried to keep up her skills—just in case.

She hesitated a moment as she remembered the last time she'd done this.

Her future had been altered—maybe permanently.

But she was willing to risk whatever she needed if it meant finding answers and helping those in desperate need of an advocate.

With that thought, she jammed the torsion wrench into the lock, along with a hook, and twisted them.

A moment later, she heard the latch click.

She released a breath.

She'd done it. The door was unlocked.

Quickly, she slipped inside.

She didn't have much time, and the massive space would take a while to search.

CHAPTER
TWENTY-SIX

DYLAN LINGERED near the hallway where Katie had disappeared.

So far, no one had spotted her.

But for how long could he say that?

He had to appear relaxed as he stood here. Otherwise, he would raise suspicions.

Thankfully, he and Brandon had already talked through their plan. They would simply act like two bored men whose dates were freshening up in the nearby restroom. It was the most logical plan of action.

Meanwhile, Finley was talking to Donovan in hopes of distracting the man for a while.

Before long, Blackout might want to consider recruiting these ladies to work for them. Both were outstanding, quick-witted, and brave.

"So, I say go hunting in Montana when the season opens . . ." Brandon said loudly.

Dylan took another sip of his drink as he listened. "Montana is the best."

They continued the conversation. When appropriate, Dylan nodded enthusiastically, hoping to make it seem like they were just two guys discussing their next adventure.

But Dylan, at every opportunity, glanced down the hallway.

Katie was still in the office.

The guard snacked on some food but still stood watch.

And Joe Faulkner still wandered the perimeter of the room. Had Donovan hired him just as security? Or was Dagger somehow a part of this too?

Either way, that guy would recognize them. Dylan felt sure of it.

Then their cover would be blown, and things would go south quickly.

"You really do like her, don't you?"

Dylan flinched as he realized Brandon was staring at him. "What?"

"Maddox was right. You like her. Katie. I can tell by the way you look at her."

Dylan shrugged. "Does it matter?"

Brandon stepped closer. "Look, if you care about her, you need to let her know who you really are."

He swallowed hard. He wished it were that simple. "If I do that, I'll blow the operation and she won't let me protect her."

Brandon narrowed his gaze. "I'm saying this as someone who's been in your shoes before. It's not going to end well if you keep secrets from her."

Dylan frowned. He knew exactly what Brandon was talking about.

Brandon had met and fallen in love with Finley while on an undercover assignment in Ecuador. When she'd learned the truth about who he really was, she'd vowed to never forgive him.

Thankfully, that had changed. But no one would have blamed Finley if she hadn't forgiven him. She'd felt betrayed, and rightfully so.

Dylan knew without a doubt that Katie would feel the same.

More turmoil churned inside him.

The security guard touched his earpiece and spoke into his mic. Then he turned and hurried down the hallway toward the office.

All those troubles were forgotten in an instant.

What if this guy caught Katie?

Katie decided to start with Donovan's desk.

It seemed like the most logical place to begin.

She riffled through the files and papers on top first, but she didn't see anything of interest.

Next, she went through the drawers.

Still nothing incriminating.

Of course. Donovan was too smart for that.

So where would he leave any kind of information he didn't want to be found?

He could be keeping it strictly digital.

But that was also risky. Anything electronic could be breached, even if it was encrypted.

Printing out details of illegal operations also seemed risky.

Donovan was sneaky. Whatever information he had on illegal projects would be disguised.

Katie glanced around again, knowing she didn't have much time.

Several filing cabinets stood behind her, but they would take hours to look through.

Instead, she sat down in his chair and glanced at his desktop.

A large calendar stretched there. Apparently, Donovan was old school and still liked to write down appointments on paper. She quickly took a picture of his schedule just in case she needed it later.

As she did, she leaned closer.

Katie could barely make out the indentation of some words that had been written on another paper, leaving a faint impression in the calendar.

She grabbed a pencil to see if she could uncover them.

But, before she could start, her phone buzzed.

It was Dylan.

Security guard coming your way.

Just as she read the message, she heard the door handle twist.

CHAPTER
TWENTY-SEVEN

DYLAN STARTED to rush down the hallway when a hand clamped his bicep.

"Just give it time," Brandon said quietly.

Dylan's muscles remained rigid. The last thing he wanted was for Katie to be stuck in that room with that security guard. If she was caught, he had no doubt the man would be ruthless.

And then there was Donovan . . . that man seemed like pure danger.

"She's got this," Brandon continued. "Katie is one tough cookie. She's been in war zones and in the middle of riots. If I remember correctly, she was even in Iraq right before the militants took over. She can handle this."

Dylan knew that Brandon was probably right. But

still, he didn't like the idea of her being in there alone. He wanted to be closer. To help.

His phone buzzed, and he glanced down. His breath caught when he saw a text from Katie.

I'm okay. Hiding.

Brandon peered over his shoulder. "See, I told you she was fine."

Katie's words might be true for now. But if that guard didn't come out within the next few minutes, Dylan would think of an excuse to barge in there.

"Looks like we have other trouble," Brandon said.

Dylan dragged his gaze away from the office and glanced in the direction Brandon stared.

His lungs tightened when he saw Joe Faulkner walking through the crowd toward them.

"Do you think he's seen us?" Dylan asked.

"Doesn't seem like he's been close enough to us to have seen us. But he's definitely coming this way. If he spots us . . . this whole thing is blown."

More tension rose in Dylan.

He glanced back at the office door.

The guard still hadn't emerged. Dylan didn't dare to text Katie just in case her phone vibrated and gave away her presence.

As Dylan glanced back at the crowd, he saw Joe

cutting through everyone as he headed in their direction.

The smart thing to do right now would be to hide before Joe saw him or Brandon.

But that would mean leaving Katie by herself.

That wasn't something Dylan could bring himself to do.

———

Katie pulled her legs to her chest as she curled into a ball beneath Donovan's massive wooden desk.

This wasn't her first rodeo. She'd certainly been in ugly situations before. Usually, for the sake of getting a story.

The thing was . . . her stories were never about herself. Never because she wanted the acclaim and glory that went with the big headlines.

But the leads she chased directly affected other people. She needed to bring awareness to world events so others could intercede and help. Most people didn't understand that about her.

This was no different.

She'd read up on everything she could find about the prevalence of trafficking in today's world. She knew that Donovan had *something* to do with it.

Needless to say, he was somehow profiting off innocent, helpless people.

The thought caused anger to burn through her.

Footsteps sounded behind her.

The security guard lingered on the other side of the desk.

Only inches away from her.

Only separated by a thin sheet of wood.

She held her breath, desperate not to make any sounds.

"It looks clear," the man said, probably into a comm. "But the door was cracked slightly."

Cracked slightly? Katie had closed it behind her, hadn't she? Maybe she hadn't latched it.

Rookie mistake, she chided herself.

"Yeah, you're right. It should be locked. I'll take another look around." Shuffling sounded before the man muttered, "Idiot."

As Katie glanced down, she saw the man's shadow. The door in the background was open, casting light into the room.

She hoped that didn't somehow illuminate her. She didn't think that it would. As long as the man didn't pull the chair out and look beneath the desk, she should be okay.

He continued pacing before pausing on the far side of the desk.

What had triggered him to look inside the office? The cracked door?

Or had she set off some type of alarm?

But Katie found that hard to believe. She hadn't seen any indications this office was secured by anything but the locked door.

Had there been a security camera hidden in the office?

If that was the case, she was already a sitting duck, and this man was just playing games with her.

Her heart beat harder.

The guard crossed to the front of the desk, to where the chair was.

Katie could see him clearly. See his shiny black shoes. His pressed black pants.

See the gun in the holster at his waist.

Was he about to discover her?

She didn't know.

Katie pressed her eyes closed and prayed she'd get out of here alive.

TWENTY-EIGHT

DYLAN TURNED SO Joe wouldn't see his face. But where he and Brandon were standing, there was nowhere to hide. Instead, he took out his cell phone and held it up. Except, instead of searching for something on the phone, he turned the camera on, making it so the lens faced him.

It gave Dylan the chance to watch Joe without Joe seeing his face.

For a while, at least.

He observed the man's image on the screen.

In ten more feet, Joe would reach them.

How would he and Brandon explain their presence here?

As soon as Joe knew who they were, he'd report them to Donovan.

If Katie wasn't trapped inside the office, Dylan

would get out of here before he received unnecessary attention.

It was a trick he'd learned doing covert operations: only make a scene when necessary. Otherwise, be a ghost.

But that wasn't an option right now.

There was no way he was leaving her behind.

At just that moment, a group of partygoers started toward the door, forming a blockade of sorts.

Dylan saw Joe stop on the other side of the crowd.

Several people called out hello to him. One lady paused near Joe, making small talk, and maybe even flirting.

Dylan and Brandon glanced at each other.

That had bought them a little time.

But soon, these people would be on their way.

As the last person in the group trickled toward the door, Dylan saw Joe step closer.

Before the man reached them, his radio buzzed. Joe placed his hand at his ear as if listening and responding through an in-ear comm.

Then, with one more glance at them, he turned and headed back into the party.

He'd clearly been called away for something.

Dylan felt his shoulders soften.

At least one problem was taken care of.

For now.

But that guard had been in there with Katie for a long time.

If she didn't come out in another sixty seconds, Dylan would have to go in.

———

Katie continued to pray she wouldn't be found. But the man remained by the desk. All he had to do was pull that chair out and . . .

Suddenly, he moved again.

A little closer.

Let out a grunt.

The next instant, he took a step back.

He was heading back toward the door.

But Katie wasn't ready to let her guard down yet.

She heard the door open wider. Then she heard a click.

The light disappeared from the room as the door shut.

She remained where she was, needing certainty that the man was gone.

After counting to twenty, she pressed herself into the floor and glanced beneath the desk.

She didn't see any shoes or legs anywhere in the room.

It looked like the man had really left.

Katie pushed the chair out of the way, scanned the office, and saw it was clear.

Working quickly, she grabbed the pencil again and gently ran it over the calendar. It seemed like the oldest trick in the book, one she'd read about in mystery novels as she was growing up.

But it worked.

A name appeared.

New Life Enterprises.

She took a picture of the calendar with her phone. Then she erased her pencil marks, wiped the eraser residue into her hand, and tossed it in the trashcan. She returned the desk to the way she'd found it.

Now, it was time for her to get out of here.

She just had to make sure the security guard didn't see her leave.

She grabbed her phone and texted Dylan.

Need to get out. Can you distract the guard?

Then she waited for his response.

JUST AS DYLAN took a step down the hallway, the door opened.

He froze and watched as the security guard stepped out.

Alone.

Dylan wanted to feel relief. But that emotion seemed premature.

As the man reached the start of the hallway, Dylan's phone buzzed.

It was Katie.

He quickly read her message and then glanced around.

"She needs a distraction so she can get out," he told Brandon.

Brandon raised his chin. "I've got this. Tell her to give me ten seconds, and then she can come out."

Dylan texted Katie the message.

When he hit Send, Brandon walked toward the guard with his drink in hand. His steps seemed flimsy and uneven.

He was pretending to be inebriated, Dylan realized.

The next instant, Brandon tumbled toward the guard. His drink spilled all over the man's shirt.

"Oh, man!" Brandon said a little too loudly. "I am so sorry. I don't even know what happened . . ."

The security guard looked at him with narrowed eyes and a gaze that could kill. "You idiot."

"I'll pay to have that dry-cleaned, man." He pulled a tissue from his pocket and began to blot the man's suit—ensuring the man was turned away from the hallway. "Let me get you some soda water or something."

"You've done plenty . . ."

As Brandon hassled with the man, the door to the office opened.

Katie slunk out. She pressed herself against the wall before slipping past the guard and reaching Dylan. She took his arm and pulled him to the door.

"I think it's time we get out of here," she muttered.

Dylan couldn't think of a single thing he wanted to do more.

It took several minutes for the valet to return their car.

Katie couldn't wait to get inside and away from this place. She'd found what she needed, and now she knew without a doubt staying here any longer would be dangerous. Someone was willing to kill her if she found out too much information.

She didn't think it mattered if they killed her in her home, at the university, or even at this party. These guys were the types who'd make up an excuse about how she was a threat. How they had no choice but to pull the trigger.

Since money could talk, Donovan would certainly get away with it. Katie had no doubt about that.

Finally, she and Dylan were in his SUV and heading down the street. Maybe she could finally breathe easier, for a little while at least.

"So?" Dylan glanced at her.

"First of all, thank you for that. You're amazing at subterfuge. So, if you decide not to be an assistant one day, then maybe you should look into—"

"Being your sidekick?" he quickly filled in.

Katie smiled. "I was going to say you could become a bodyguard. Being my sidekick doesn't sound that bad either."

He flashed her a grin. "So, what did you find out?"

She shared with him the name she had seen on the calendar—New Life Enterprises.

"Does that mean anything to you?"

She shook her head. "Not really. But I'm going to see what I can find out. I know this could be nothing. But it could be something. Plus, I took a picture of his calendar, so I know all of Donovan's upcoming appointments. I figured that could prove useful also."

"Good work, Katie."

For some reason, Dylan's affirmation made her feel a measure of delight. It wasn't often she wanted the approval of others. In fact, she was proud of herself for not caring if she had other people's support. But something about Dylan was different.

As light flooded the console in front of her, she glanced behind her and saw that a car had pulled up behind them. The driver seemed too close, especially for this narrow, winding country road.

She glanced at Dylan and saw his gaze harden.

That's when she realized they were still in trouble.

The car behind them . . . its close proximity wasn't an accident.

Someone was following them.

"Dylan . . . I shouldn't have brought you into this." Katie glanced at him again, hating that she'd put him in this position.

He gripped the steering wheel tighter and murmured, "I've got this. Hold on."

That's when Katie knew she was in for the ride of her life.

DYLAN SHOULD HAVE KNOWN that was too easy.

No doubt, Joe had seen them at the party. Maybe Joe didn't recognize him and Brandon, but the man was certainly still suspicious. Joe could have also looked at security camera footage and seen what they were up to.

If Donovan knew Katie had been there and had slipped into his office, he'd realize she was looking for dirt.

That meant there was no way he'd let her get away.

The car sped up behind them until the headlights disappeared from sight.

"Dylan . . ." Katie grasped the handle above the door and her other hand gripped the armrest.

"Hold on." Dylan jammed on the accelerator.

His SUV was good and solid.

But it wasn't as fast as the car behind him.

The next instant, something nudged them.

The other driver had hit them!

The tension between his shoulders stretched even tauter.

He glanced ahead and saw an upcoming curve.

There was no way he could take that turn going eighty miles an hour.

The SUV would tip.

He swallowed hard and tapped into his defensive driving skills.

Before he could slow down, the car rammed his bumper again. This time a little harder.

He glanced in the rearview mirror again and saw the headlights had disappeared.

He braced himself for another impact.

The car nudged his SUV again, propelling them forward.

"Watch out!" Katie's voice trembled with fear.

As he approached the hairpin turn, he lifted a prayer.

Just as he started to jerk the steering wheel to the left, the car clipped his bumper.

The SUV fishtailed.

Dylan tugged at the steering wheel, trying to counteract the sudden swerve.

His vehicle tilted, threatening to roll before it veered off the road and tumbled onto the grassy embankment.

Katie let out a scream as they bumped across the dirt, going entirely too fast.

Then abruptly, they lurched forward as the car suddenly stopped.

The hood crumpled.

Airbags deployed.

Dust filled the air.

Then silence.

A tree.

They'd hit a tree.

———

Katie felt dazed as the world stopped around her.

"Are you okay?" Dylan peered at her.

She wasn't sure. Her head was still spinning. "I . . . I think so."

"We've got to move," he rushed. "Now."

He pressed her seatbelt buckle until it released. Then he climbed out and darted to her side of the SUV. He jerked the door open, took her hand, and pulled her out before she even realized what was happening.

She briefly caught a glimpse of the car that had run them off the road. It idled close by, headlights shining into the distance.

Dylan tugged on her arm. "Let's go."

She saw the rumpled front side of Dylan's SUV as they ran past it and into the woods.

He kept running, deeper into the cover of trees. Katie could hardly even see in front of her. But she just ran, letting Dylan pull her behind him as they darted through the darkness.

Footsteps sounded behind them.

Shouts filled the air.

The men who'd run them off the road weren't far behind.

Her heart pounded harder at the thought.

She wanted to slow down, to catch her breath.

But she knew that wasn't an option.

Branches slapped her face. Underbrush tugged at her dress. Rocks tried to twist her ankles.

But adrenaline—and Dylan—kept her moving forward.

As she skittered down a rocky embankment, her foot landed sideways and twisted.

She let out a gasp.

Dylan glanced back and must have seen the pain

on her face.

He quickly took in their surroundings.

The next instant, he swept her into his arms and stashed her behind a cluster of trees.

He knelt beside her and put his finger to his lips, indicating for her to be quiet.

Katie quickly nodded.

She had no choice but to remain silent, despite her throbbing ankle. Her heavy breathing. Her trembling.

She couldn't make a sound.

Not if they wanted to survive.

The men still pounded through the forest. They were moving. Shouting. Searching for them like dogs on a coon hunt.

Dylan grabbed a large rock beside him and peered around the trees again.

A moment later, he drew his arm back and tossed the rock across the woods.

The men chasing them seemed to pause.

"Did you hear that?" one of them asked.

"They're over there!"

The men took off toward the sound.

Brilliant thinking, Dylan. But Katie didn't dare say the words aloud.

As the men moved farther away, Dylan knelt in front of her again.

"That will buy us a little bit of time," he whispered. "How is your ankle?"

He reached for her leg and felt the skin around the area.

As he did, fire raced through Katie's blood.

Not because he'd hurt her. But because of his warm, strong, and reassuring touch.

Did he even know he had that effect on her? Did he realize that when he'd almost kissed her, the entire world had disappeared for a moment?

She wasn't sure that had ever happened before.

Her mind was always working. Always thinking. Always aware of the things around her.

Except for ten seconds tonight when she'd been swept away.

"I think it's okay." Katie tried to move her foot to get a better assessment. She could rotate her ankle slightly. "It's not broken. I just twisted it."

His gaze locked on hers. "Do you think you can make it any farther?"

"I don't think we have much choice. Those guys might circle back around here."

"My thoughts too." He pulled out his phone. "I have service. We need some backup. I'm going to text Brandon and see where he is."

"How is Brandon going to help us?" Dylan was giving his friend a little too much credit. He might be ex-military, but this didn't exactly fit a normal military operation.

They didn't have guns or any other survival gear, for starters.

"Brandon is very resourceful." Dylan's fingers moved across the phone screen. "Plus, if I'm reading this map correctly, there's a street on the other side of these woods. If Brandon can come and pick us up there . . ."

She hadn't thought of that scenario. That sounded much better than fighting blind in the dark woods.

Katie didn't argue. She didn't have any better ideas.

As soon as Dylan sent the text, the voices in the distance became louder.

Dylan tugged her shoes off. "You okay running barefoot?"

She nodded. "Yes."

"Perfect. Because we need to move."

Katie gritted her teeth, pushing aside the pain as Dylan helped her to her feet.

Then they darted through the woods again.

DYLAN KEPT a tight grip on Katie's hand. The two of them couldn't afford to lose any more time.

By his estimations, four men were chasing them.

Most likely, they were guards who'd been at the party. Not like the one at the hallway entrance, who was more like a rent-a-cop figure.

These guys were probably with Dagger.

That meant they were extremely dangerous. Skilled. Deadly.

Thankfully, these woods weren't that big, and Dylan had an idea of which way to run to get to the road—where, hopefully, Brandon would find them.

But if he wasn't careful, his cover would be blown.

Katie was fast behind him, but not as fast as she

could be. Her ankle held her back, as well as her dress and her bare feet.

They were going to have to work with those limitations.

They didn't have any other options right now.

"Hey!" someone yelled in the distance.

Then a light shone on them.

They'd been spotted.

The next instant, gunfire filled the air.

He dove, his body covering Katie's as they hit the ground with an *umph*.

"Are you hit?" he whispered.

Katie shook her head no, even though he felt her trembling beneath him.

"We can't stay here," he said. "Our chances are better if we keep moving."

Her gaze almost looked stormy as she nodded again. "Okay."

Dylan grabbed her hand. On the count of three, he pulled her to her feet, and they darted across the landscape again.

Footsteps pounded.

Sticks cracked.

More shots rang out in the nighttime air.

Wood splintered on a tree beside them.

They kept moving.

Just ahead, Dylan saw lights.

Headlights?

Was that Brandon?

Or could this be another car full of men with guns determined to kill them?

It looked like they were about to find out.

———

Everything was happening so fast Katie hardly had time to think.

She supposed she'd have time for that later.

If they survived.

She saw two lights in front of her and wondered if they were headlights. She dared hope they were from Brandon's vehicle.

What were the odds he could have gotten here this quickly?

As she and Dylan got closer, she realized the lights were from a car.

Dylan paused at the edge of the woods before pulling her faster. "It's Brandon. He's here."

The next instant, they shot out of the woods and dove into the backseat of the waiting SUV.

As Dylan slammed the door shut behind them, Brandon took off down the road.

Had this really just happened?

Everything almost seemed surreal.

Except Katie's throbbing ankle served as a stark reminder this was real.

She took several deep breaths, trying to calm herself. But it did no good.

She'd just been chased by armed thugs through the woods. And Dylan had seemed to know just what to do.

Who was this guy anyway?

She glanced in the front seat at Brandon and Finley. Brandon gripped the steering wheel tight as he drove, while Finley glanced back at them in concern.

Katie's adrenaline seemed to fade, and, in an instant, trembles consumed her.

Dylan reached in the back and pulled out a blanket, draping it around her bare shoulders. "We're safe now. Are you okay?"

Katie stared at him, questions suddenly hitting her at full force. Not just questions.

Realizations.

Why in the world would an assistant at a university have those kinds of survival skills?

Sure, Dylan had been in the military. But there was more behind Dylan's actions than that.

How had he known Brandon kept a blanket in the back of his SUV? Come to think of it, Brandon's SUV was the same make and model as Dylan's.

Was that a coincidence?

Katie was certain something more was going on here.

Brandon had found them like a pro.

"Katie?" Dylan repeated.

She pulled herself back to the present. She would deal with these questions in a moment. Right now, they still needed to get far away from those guys.

"I'm fine. My ankle's sore, but I will be okay. You?"

Dylan continued to study her face, his handsome features full of concern.

Gentle warrior, she thought.

That's how she would describe Dylan.

"I'm fine," Dylan told her. "But that was close back there."

"You don't have to tell me." She pulled the blanket tighter across her shoulders and glanced at Brandon and Finley in the front seat. "I'm glad you guys were here ready and waiting for us."

"We left a few minutes behind you," Brandon said. "We saw your car on the side of the road. Then when I got the text from Dylan . . . I'm glad we got here when we did."

More truths tried to click into place in Katie's mind.

She held them at bay. Timing was everything.

And, right now, she had other more important things to deal with.

"Should we call the police?" she asked.

Brandon and Dylan exchanged another silent glance.

"I'll call when I get back to the apartment," Dylan finally said. "We can't afford to hang around here any longer to give our statements. It can wait."

"You're right," Katie said. "Those guys wanted to kill us. Did they follow us from the party?"

"They did," Brandon said. "I saw Joe talking to a couple of guys after you left. A few minutes later, they ran out the door like something was on fire."

"Joe?" she asked. "Who's Joe?"

Dylan and Brandon glanced at each other again. The look was subtle, but she saw the unspoken conversation between them.

"Joe was one of the security guards at the party." Brandon made the statement with ease, like it was no big deal that he knew that.

Other people may have passed it off as nothing—but not Katie. She knew there was something she was missing.

"How do you know his first name?" she prodded.

"I talked to him," Brandon said. "I was trying to buy some time while you were in the office. The guy seemed shady."

Katie didn't fully buy his explanation.

But she still waited, knowing that patience was a better virtue than anger right now.

These guys had saved her life.

She didn't exactly want to tear into them with her words.

But anger began to bubble inside her.

Someone wasn't telling the truth.

Someone in this car.

And it wasn't Katie.

DYLAN STUDIED KATIE'S FACE.

She knew something was going on, didn't she?

He'd known it was only a matter of time before the woman figured things out. She was a smart lady.

Tonight had brought out Dylan's tactical skills. He couldn't help but use them—not if he wanted to stay alive.

He knew that also meant Katie would have a lot of questions.

He could stick to his cover story and say those skills were because he'd been in the military. And, mostly, that was true. But there was more to it.

Dylan didn't want to lie to her anymore.

Especially when he remembered what Brandon had told him earlier.

Brandon and Finley's relationship had almost

been irreparably harmed after what happened to them in Ecuador. Dylan didn't want that to be the case for him and Katie.

He knew the two of them were just starting to get to know each other. It was too soon to know if they had something that would last.

But he thought they might have something that was worth a shot.

In the short time Dylan had known Katie, he'd begun to care about her. To admire her. To respect her.

Dylan hadn't felt that way about someone in a long time.

Since Rachel.

His heart let out an involuntary ache at the memory of his wife.

What would she think about all this? Would she approve of his attraction to Katie? Would she want Dylan to move on? Or would she want him to believe that the two of them had been meant to be together and there was no one else for him?

Dylan thought he knew the answer, but his emotions tangled with his logic.

———

They finally reached the apartment complex.

Katie wanted to tell Brandon to take her back to her own house. But she knew she wouldn't be safe there.

She could stay with a friend, but then she'd only be putting someone else in danger.

Her father? He was always a possibility. But he worried about her too much, and he already had so much on his plate.

Besides, Katie didn't want to walk away from this without a conversation with Dylan. She *had* to know the truth. She needed more time with him. One-on-one time where they could talk. Really talk.

Katie waited until they were out of the SUV, and Brandon and Finley drove away before saying, "Dylan, I need to know something."

As they stepped into the lobby, Dylan turned to her. "What's that?"

"Who are you really?" Anger sparked inside her. "Don't lie to me anymore."

Dylan ran a hand through his hair. Then he glanced around as if to make sure that no one else was listening before turning back to her.

"It's complicated," he said.

At least, he didn't deny it.

Katie crossed her arms. "I can understand complicated. Try me."

Dylan reached for her hand. But as he grasped it, Katie flinched, and he released her.

He frowned and let out a breath before saying, "I'm a security agent. I work for an organization called Blackout."

Katie's heart beat harder into her chest. "A security agent? Like a bodyguard?"

He raised a shoulder in a half shrug. "Something like that. Your father was worried about you and—"

"Wait. My father is a part of this?" Blood rushed through her ears.

Dylan frowned again. "He's been concerned about your safety, and you refused his offer of hiring professional protection for you, so . . ."

"He hired you. A bodyguard. Somehow, he got you a job at the university as my assistant, and then he told you to pass yourself off as a meek and mild Clark Kent?" Nausea—and disgust—churned in her gut. How could she have fallen for it?

"It's not that simple." Dylan rubbed his jaw.

"But, in a nutshell, that's what it is, right?"

He hesitated a moment before nodding. "I suppose."

"You don't even really need to wear glasses do you?"

"No, I don't."

More fire raced through her blood, and she began pacing. "I can't believe this."

"Your father didn't want you to get hurt."

She turned to him, flames flickering in her gaze. "Tell me who you really are. What else have you lied to me about? Rachel? Were you really married, or was that all part of your façade to earn my trust?"

"Katie . . ." Dylan started to reach for her again but caught himself and dropped his hand. "I wouldn't lie about that. All I lied about was why I'm really here, but I tried to keep the rest of the details about my life true. I don't like deceiving people. Believe me, I don't."

She shook her head. "I can't trust you anymore. People who lie about one thing will lie about anything."

"It's not that I wanted to keep this from you." He lowered his voice. "But your father's main concern was your safety."

More fire lit in her gaze. "Don't you worry—I'll have words for my father as well. Right now, I just want to get back to my house."

His eyes widened. "That's not a good idea. I know you're angry but—"

"I'm *more* than angry."

Dylan raised his palm as if trying to calm her down. "I understand. You have every right to be. Just stay at my apartment tonight until we can figure out somewhere else you can be safe. When your father learns that I told you the truth, I'll probably be fired anyway. I don't have anything left to lose. But I just need to know you'll be safe. Please."

She stared at him another moment, her mind still racing. He sounded sincere. And he had just saved her life back in the woods.

But she still had more questions.

"What about Brandon? Maddox? Are they with this Blackout organization also?"

Dylan nodded.

Her irritation only grew stronger. "What about Finley?"

"She really is Brandon's girlfriend, and she really is the CEO of Embolden."

"At least that's something." Katie stared at him another moment as she contemplated what she should do.

She wanted to walk away. To erase this part of her life.

But, unfortunately, life was never that easy.

DYLAN STARED at Katie as he waited to hear what else she had to say. He prayed she wouldn't walk away right now.

It wouldn't be safe.

Plus, he wasn't ready for her to be out of his life. He still had things he needed to explain. Maybe with some time, she would understand . . .

"I'll stay here tonight, and then I'll figure out what to do next," Katie finally said. "But I *hate* being lied to."

"I don't blame you. I do too. I never thought when I took this job—"

She raised her hand, motioning for him to stop. "Whatever your explanation is, save it. I don't want to hear any more excuses. Now, if it's okay, I'm tired and I'd like to get to bed."

Dylan stared at her another moment, all the words he wanted to say dying on his tongue. Instead, he nodded.

Katie hobbled beside him as they walked to his apartment. No doubt, painful cuts and scrapes stretched across her feet and legs from their run through the forest. In other circumstances, he would help her clean those wounds and try to ease her discomfort.

But Dylan knew Katie wouldn't want anything to do with him right now.

He understood why. But what he hadn't anticipated was the sting that brought along with it.

Katie was quiet as Dylan unlocked the apartment door and they slipped inside.

He glanced in the living room and noted that Connie must have already gone to bed. But Maddox sat on the couch, still crocheting beanies while watching a fight on TV.

Katie scowled at Maddox before slipping past him and down the hallway toward her room.

When Dylan glanced back at Maddox, he saw the questions in his colleague's gaze.

"Guess that didn't go well," his friend muttered.

Dylan scowled as he dropped onto the couch and let his head fall back against the cushions. "You could say that."

He gave Maddox a quick update of the night's events.

Maddox continued crocheting as he listened, his stitches slowing and quickening with different parts of the story. "I'm sorry, man. That sounds rough."

Dylan let out a sigh, realizing he needed to change the subject. He needed to process the turn of events with Katie internally before speaking them out loud anymore.

"Any problems here?" he asked instead.

"It's been quiet. No complaints."

"That's good news, at least." Dylan resisted a sigh.

He wasn't ready to walk away from this investigation. He now felt just as committed as Katie.

However, Dylan knew that chances were Katie would never want to see him again. He most likely would be fired from this job, and he'd return to Lantern Beach.

But none of that felt right in his gut. Dylan had started this assignment, and he desperately wanted to complete it. He wanted to make things right.

Now he just needed to figure out a way to ensure he could.

Because if something happened to Katie because of his deception, Dylan wouldn't ever forgive himself.

Katie was still stewing over everything she'd learned.

When she'd gotten back to her room, she saw Connie was sleeping soundly.

Quietly, Katie had stripped off her ruined dress and stepped into the shower. As the water hit her skin, her ankle burned.

Not only was her injured ankle swollen, but cuts and scrapes sliced up her legs, reminders of what had happened tonight. At least, this was her only injury—unless she included her heart.

It surprisingly felt shattered. How had she let herself get so close to Dylan so fast? It was unlike her.

And a mistake.

A huge mistake.

She finished in the shower, dressed, and found a first aid kit to use in bandaging herself.

Her ankle still ached, but she hoped if she propped her leg up tonight that it would feel better in the morning. She found a couple of pain relievers, popped them in her mouth, and downed them with a bottle of water.

An ice pack for her ankle sounded good, but there was no way she'd go out there and risk seeing Dylan again—not unless she absolutely had to.

No, right now, she just wanted to be alone to fume over how other people acted as if she were naive and delicate.

What had her father been thinking hiring protection for her behind her back? And then making Dylan deceive her into believing he was an assistant?

It wasn't that Katie was invincible, but she wasn't made of porcelain either. She could look out for herself. If she wanted someone protecting her, she could have hired them.

But all this had been done in secret.

The thought made her feel foolish. Here she was an investigative journalist, yet she'd let the wool be pulled over her eyes.

It was disgraceful.

As were her feelings for Dylan. She'd known better. But she'd honestly thought there could be something between them. She'd allowed herself to have hope.

Now she realized that she'd been so, so wrong.

Tension knotted her muscles at the thought, tension that only grew tighter the more she ruminated over it.

Dressed in her pajamas, she sat on her bed and grabbed her computer. She typed in "New Life Enterprises" and waited to see what popped up.

Maybe doing something she was good at would

make her feel better about the things she had been tricked into believing.

She frowned.

She could hope, at least.

THE NEXT MORNING, Dylan felt the full effects of his sleepless night as he sat at the kitchen table and sipped his coffee.

All night, he'd wondered about Katie. Wondered what she was thinking. How she was feeling. How today would go.

He'd already called Mr. Logan and explained the situation.

Dylan wasn't sure if he should let Katie talk to her father first but, since Mr. Logan had hired him, it only seemed right that Dylan broke the news.

Mr. Logan hadn't been happy, but he also hadn't been surprised. According to Mr. Logan, he'd known it would only be a matter of time until his daughter put things together. He promised to talk to her later and see if he could smooth things out, but he expected Dylan to stay on the case until he heard back.

At eight a.m., Katie emerged from her bedroom.

Dylan rose from his seat and braced himself for whatever she would say.

Instead, she breezed past him, giving him the cold shoulder as she grabbed a disposable cup and filled it with coffee.

He should have expected the reaction. But it still stung.

She pressed the lid on before turning toward him. Any of the affection that had previously been in her eyes was now gone.

"I'm going to pack my things, and I'll be staying at my house from now on," she stated.

Dylan's chest muscles tightened. "Katie . . . it's not safe."

"Do you know what's not safe? Being with people you can't trust." She cast him an accusatory glance.

"You've got to believe me. I didn't want to lie to you."

"I don't have to believe anything." Her eyes remained hard.

Dylan stared at her another moment before nodding. He knew he didn't have a leg to stand on right now. But if Katie did go to her house, he'd simply park himself outside so he could keep an eye on things. She couldn't stop him from doing that.

Unless she called the police and told them Dylan was stalking her. Would she take things that far?

He had no idea how this would play out. But he had one more angle he might be able to work. It was worth a shot—especially considering everything that was on the line.

He stared down at Katie. "What about Connie?"

Katie shrugged. "What about her?"

"If you don't want protection, then who will keep an eye on her?"

Doubt filled her gaze. She hadn't thought about that, had she?

Hope ballooned inside him.

But just as quickly, Katie raised her chin. "Maybe I can talk my father into hiring you to protect her."

"But you know the two of you go hand in hand," Dylan reminded her. "That you're connected."

She narrowed her gaze, her shoulders seeming to sag. "I can't let anything happen to my cousin. You know that."

Dylan stared at her. "Then you're going to need to make up your mind. Am I going to keep working as your security detail? Or are you going to face the danger on your own and hope nothing happens to Connie?"

———

Katie mulled over Dylan's words.

He was playing dirty, and she didn't like it. Still, she knew she couldn't do anything to put Connie at risk. It was one thing to be stubbornly determined when your own life was on the line. But Connie was far more naive than Katie. She needed someone to watch her back.

Katie stared at Dylan a moment and crossed her arms, hating that he had the upper hand here. "Fine. I won't insist that my father fire you. But that doesn't mean I'm going to make this easy on you either."

A glimmer of satisfaction flitted through his gaze. "I'd expect nothing less."

"And Connie is going to call in sick to work today. It's better if she doesn't go."

"I agree."

"Meanwhile, I'm going to head into the university. And I'm not going to ride with you—not that you have a vehicle right now."

"Someone from Blackout is going to bring another vehicle. It should be here within the next hour."

He'd thought of everything, hadn't he?

"If you want to follow me there, then so be it. If you want to act as my assistant for the day, then so be it. But I'm not going to like any part of this."

Dylan stared at her, his lips flickering down in a frown. "Katie . . . I'm—"

She raised her hand in a Stop motion. She would *not* let those puppy dog eyes of his sway her decision.

Maybe he was sincere.

But she couldn't let that make a difference.

"Whatever you do, please don't apologize." She grabbed her purse and headed out the door.

A couple of seconds later, she heard Dylan's footsteps behind her. To his credit, he didn't speak. He only followed and watched their surroundings.

Like the good bodyguard he was.

She climbed into her car and started down the road for the twenty-minute drive to the university. When she glanced in the mirror, she spotted Dylan. He must have borrowed Maddox's SUV, and she assumed Maddox would use the new vehicle.

As she drove, she dialed her father's number.

Katie might as well get this conversation out of the way.

From the sullen tone of her dad's voice when he answered, she could tell he already knew what she was calling about. Dylan must have given him the update.

"How could you do this to me?" she started.

"Katie . . . because I love you. I couldn't stand the thought of something happening to you."

She didn't let the concern in her father's voice break her resolve. "It wasn't your decision to make."

"You wouldn't accept the help I offered. So, I had to get creative."

"Dad . . ." She didn't even know how to argue with him, especially since his reasoning was love. Finally, she said, "I *am* an adult."

"But you'll always be my baby. If you have kids one day, you'll understand. Don't be too hard on him."

Katie bristled at her father's words. "Don't be too hard on Dylan? Why shouldn't I be?"

"He wanted to come clean with you, but I told him he couldn't. He didn't like deceiving you."

Tension embedded itself in her back. "Like it or not, that's what he did."

"Just give it some time, and maybe you'll see more clearly. I think you need his protection, Katie."

She drew in a deep breath, willing herself to remain civil. "I told him I wouldn't ask you to fire him, but I won't be his buddy anymore either."

"I guess that's better than nothing."

Katie's shoulders stiffened. "You guess?"

"You need time to think this through."

She wished she believed her dad. Believed that after some time had passed maybe she'd see more clearly and feel more forgiving and understanding.

But Katie couldn't see that happening.

THIRTY-FIVE

DYLAN SAT at his desk grading some assignments Katie had left for him. She seemed to have given him an extra allotment of work today. She might even be getting some enjoyment out of piling on the tedious assignments.

He hated the new coldness to her gaze and the aloofness of her presence. She was angry—and rightfully so. But Dylan didn't know how to make that better. He'd apologized, but that clearly wasn't enough.

Brandon had warned him that this would happen. Dylan hadn't doubted his friend's words. But now he had no idea what to do about it.

While Katie took lunch in her office, Dylan decided to do more research into New Life Enterprises. He'd done some last night but hadn't found any answers. He had no doubt Katie was also looking into the company, but she hadn't mentioned anything.

Earlier, he'd called the Blackout headquarters and asked Colton to see what he could find out about the corporation. There was surprisingly little to be found about them online. Then again, maybe that *wasn't* so surprising.

Donovan Sullivan seemed like a sneaky kind of guy.

Just as Dylan's break ended, Colton called him back.

"I have two updates for you," he stated.

Dylan hoped whatever Colton was about to say proved useful. He knew in his gut that they were running out of time.

"I think I found some information on New Life Enterprises. It was registered as a business by Donovan Sullivan and one of his employees named Marvin Pearsall. I also found an address affiliated with the company—according to the official paper-work they filed with the state, at least." As Colton rattled off the address, Dylan jotted it down.

He stared at it a moment.

The location was local.

He wanted to check it out. But he was certain that Katie would also want to investigate.

That meant he needed to decide exactly how to handle that.

"Did you check it out?" Dylan asked.

"No, we're working another assignment right now. But we can head there tomorrow."

Dylan stored away that information, knowing that tomorrow wouldn't be soon enough for Katie.

"Second thing," Colton continued. "I sent Brandon and Titus to that farm where you saw Kingston and his crew. They were able to sneak inside after everyone left."

"And?" Dylan sat up straighter, trying not to look suspicious to anyone who might be nearby.

"It's not what you think. It turns out . . . he's making moonshine."

"What?" His shoulders slumped. They *were* in the mountains of Appalachia, an area that had been known for its moonshine at one time. But . . .

"They slipped by a couple of guards and found all the equipment, including several stills. Also found loads of ingredients. Yeast, sugar. Everything they need."

"Including the moonshine?"

"They didn't actually find the moonshine itself," Colton said. "They're assuming the guys must have loaded some trucks to deliver a shipment or something. But that's what those plastic containers were being used for."

Dylan lowered his voice. "If they're producing alcohol, why hide it? It's not illegal."

"If you don't want to pay taxes on it, then you don't announce what you're doing. Either way, it doesn't look like he's your guy here."

Dylan let that sink in. "Not what I wanted to hear. Did they report the findings?"

"Not yet. But I have a friend at the ATF that I'm going to call. I don't want to make any sudden moves."

"Understood. Thanks for the updates."

"Be careful," Colton warned. "I don't know what's going on there, but the situation is clearly just as dangerous as ever."

———

Monday was the day Katie taught her late class at 7 p.m.

Her friends often joked on her, but she loved to be in bed by nine. She'd always been that way. She woke up early and went to bed early, and she preferred that schedule. She liked having the mornings to herself to get things done in the quiet before the day began.

It hadn't been her idea to schedule an evening class, but she'd gone along with it. She figured she could do it for a year.

The lecture hall was full. Legal Issues for Journalists was one of her most popular classes. Katie liked to interject stories about experiences she'd had while reporting. In war zones. With bombs exploding in the background. How she'd been able to help a family escape over the Syrian border and find shelter in Turkey.

Sometimes those experiences seemed like a lifetime ago. But that passion to help others was still like fire in her blood.

As class ended, several students came up front to ask questions. Ordinarily, Katie wouldn't think much of it. But, given everything that happened, she felt jumpy. She didn't want to hang around any longer than she had to.

As she talked to a group of students, her gaze wandered to the back of the auditorium.

Stiles lingered there.

A shiver raced through her. Dylan said the student had an alibi for the time of one of her attacks. But she still felt uneasy around him.

She automatically looked for Dylan and found him standing at the other door, keeping an eye on her. He held a pad of paper in his hand as if trying to appear like a good assistant.

But Katie knew what he was really doing.

Although she wouldn't admit it to Dylan, she was glad he was close.

His gaze followed hers to Stiles. His shoulders became rigid at the sight of him.

Stiles glanced over at Dylan, and his eyes widened as if he were spooked.

The next moment, Stiles broke out in a run and darted from the room.

"Get back to the office," Dylan yelled before taking off after the boy.

Katie quickly excused herself from her students. Trembles overtook her as she remembered the threats she'd received and being run off the road.

She started back down the hallway to her office.

As she did, the lights above her flickered.

Her lungs seemed to seize.

She'd walked down this hallway plenty of times at this hour. These lights had never flickered before.

A footstep sounded before the hallway went completely dark.

Katie's stomach clenched as she realized none of this was a coincidence.

STILES WAS quick but not as quick as Dylan. Dylan easily caught up with him and grabbed the boy's shirt. He pushed him against the wall and then towered in front of him, sending a clear message to Stiles that he wouldn't get out of this easily.

"What are you doing?" Dylan stared him square in the eye.

Stiles raised his hands, sweat springing up across his skin. "I was just listening to Ms. Logan talk. I'm in her class. There's nothing wrong with that."

"Then why did you run?"

"Because you were staring at me, and it scared me." His voice climbed in pitch.

Dylan narrowed his eyes. "I don't buy that. Innocent people don't run when people look at them."

"You always look at me with suspicion. I don't know what to say. Maybe I'm easily frightened." His words came out faster as his pitch continued to climb.

"Do you have a thing for Ms. Logan?" Dylan asked, not breaking eye contact.

"Wait . . . what?" Stiles shook his head as if cold water had been thrown on him. "I mean, I think she's great. Is that what you're getting at?"

"Have you been stalking her?"

The student's face paled. "Stalking her? No. I just like her. As a *professor*. I want to be a journalist and do the kinds of things she's done. I want to help people. I want to expose the truth. I want to do whatever is necessary to ensure bad people don't get away with evil deeds."

"So, you're obsessed with her?"

"No." Stiles let out a sigh and rolled his eyes toward the ceiling as if praying. "I'm not obsessed with her. I just want to learn everything I can from her. I'd give anything to be able to sit down with her and ask her a million questions about how she got to where she is today. She got the raw end of the deal when she was fired. Stone Media lost one of the best."

Dylan stared at the boy another moment before

releasing him. Stiles might be socially awkward, and he might admire Katie. But he wasn't necessarily dangerous.

"Listen . . ." Stiles shifted awkwardly. "There is something I've been trying to talk to Ms. Logan about."

Dylan crossed his arms. "What's that?"

He swallowed hard as his neck muscles seemed to tighten. "My best friend is actually interning for Donovan Sullivan."

Now this guy had Dylan's attention. "Go on."

He tugged on his collar. "I've been asking him some questions because I know Mr. Sullivan is the reason Ms. Logan lost her job. I don't believe she was in the wrong with what she did, however."

"What did your best friend tell you?"

"He said Mr. Sullivan has had several private meetings in his office lately." Stiles' gaze met Dylan's. "A couple of them were with someone named Kingston Baylor."

Dylan's breath caught. "What?"

"I followed you and Ms. Logan the other day. You went to Kingston's house." Stiles shrugged sheepishly. "I just . . . I don't know. She's seemed jumpy recently, and I knew she wasn't going to let things with Donovan drop. I just wanted to help."

"Go on."

"I've been trying to tell her what my best friend said, just in case it was important—especially when I learned about the connection between the two men."

"I'll pass on that message to her. In the meantime, no following her—or anyone else, for that matter."

"Understood." Stiles practically stumbled backward. "I promise. I won't."

Dylan watched as the student hurried away.

Then Dylan headed back into the lecture hall.

He'd told Katie to go back to the office, but he wanted to double-check she wasn't still there before he left this area. She may have stayed just to spite him.

But the auditorium was empty, so Dylan headed back toward the offices. As he stepped into the hallway leading to the administrative wing, he noticed the lights were out.

Tension slithered up his spine.

He needed to find Katie.

And he needed to find her now.

———

Katie took off into a run, her sprained ankle aching with every step.

But she had to push through it. Had to do her best despite the pain.

She only made it halfway down the hallway when a figure dressed all in black emerged from a doorway in front of her. The masked man grabbed her, pressed her against the wall, and his hand covered her mouth.

"You need to back off," the man said. "How many times do I have to tell you?"

She stared at the man with wide eyes, wanting to struggle and get away. But her limbs were frozen.

"Leave it alone. Do you hear me? Back. Off."

She forced herself to nod. She didn't even know for sure what she was backing off from. Most likely, Donovan. It was just like him to send this thug to do his dirty work.

"Next time, I'm not going to be so nice," the man continued.

As footsteps echoed down the hallway, they both turned toward the sound.

Dylan appeared. "Hey!"

The man shoved Katie to the floor and sprinted away.

She pulled herself upright, her hip aching and her ankle throbbing as she moved. But she didn't care right now. Instead, she watched as the man disappeared outside.

The next instant, Dylan knelt beside her. "Are you okay?"

"I'm fine. Go get him."

He hesitated a moment before rising.

Then he took off after the man.

DYLAN DASHED toward the exit the man had disappeared through. He threw himself into the door, but it didn't budge.

He tried again with the same results.

That guy must have wedged something outside the door to prevent it from opening.

A surge of anger flashed through Dylan.

He stepped back and spotted another exit farther down.

This guy would probably be gone by the time Dylan got outside, but he had to try.

He pushed through the next door, rushed out, then froze.

He searched for signs of movement. Listened for footsteps.

But everything seemed still around him. No students lingered after class. No cars left the lot.

It almost felt eerie.

Where had that guy gone?

Dylan knew there was a possibility the man had jumped in a car and taken off. The timing would have had to be just right, but it was possible.

Just as the thought rushed through his mind, he heard someone sneeze.

He darted toward the sound.

As he passed by a mini-van, he spotted someone crouched behind it.

"Hey!" Dylan shouted.

The figure raced away.

Dylan was right on his heels.

He easily caught up with the man and tackled him. In one swift motion, Dylan turned the man over and jerked off his mask.

The face Dylan saw caused the air to leave his lungs.

"Dean Sears?"

The man raised his hands in front of his face as if blocking a punch. "Please don't hurt me. I can explain."

"You're the one who just threatened Ms. Logan?"

"It's not like that. I promise. It's not. I would never hurt her."

"Are you the one who shot at her?"

"No!" Waylon's eyes widened. "Of course not."

Dylan eased off him but kept one hand on the man's chest in case he thought about running. "Then start explaining."

"I had no choice. I was just doing what I was told." Waylon's words came out scrambled, fast.

"What does that mean?" Dylan narrowed his eyes as he studied the man.

"This guy . . . wearing all black . . . he came to my house about a week ago."

"Keep going." Dylan didn't like the sound of this.

"He said if I didn't do what he told me that there would be consequences. I could lose my job. My pension. Everything."

"He blackmailed you? What did this guy have on you?"

Waylon sneezed again. "I . . . I may have had an inappropriate relationship with one of my students. She wasn't underage. In fact, she was twenty-five. But it's against university policy for me to date a student. Somehow, this guy discovered it."

"What did he tell you to do?"

"To leave the note and knife on Katie's desk. And to give her a face-to-face message tonight. But I wouldn't have hurt her. I wouldn't have taken things that far. I swear." He shook his head rapidly.

Disgust churned in Dylan's stomach as he stared at the man and realized just how spineless the guy was. "You just made things a whole lot worse for yourself. You know that, don't you?"

Waylon nodded quickly again. "I'm in over my head, but I don't know how to get out."

Dylan eased his grip when he realized Waylon was practically cowering in front of him. The man didn't seem to pose any threat.

"Do you have any idea who this guy is?" Dylan asked. "Did you see his face?"

"No, he wore a mask—like a ski mask. I didn't recognize his voice or anything. I have no idea who he is." His voice cracked as a sob escaped. "What have I done?"

Dylan frowned.

He was going to have to call the cops. There was no way around it.

Doing so would only slow down the other plans he had for tonight.

Dylan would have to adjust his schedule. But he could still make it work.

With that thought in mind, he pulled out his phone.

———

Relief filled Katie when she saw Dylan step through the doorway into the dark hallway. She stood pressed against the wall, waiting for him to reappear, and trying to keep her promise to stay where she was.

But every sound had made her jump. She could hardly breathe as she waited for Dylan. She'd prayed that he was okay. That he hadn't gotten hurt on her account.

When she spotted the man with Dylan, she sucked in a breath.

Was that . . . Dean Sears?

"Do you want to tell her, or do you want me to?" Dylan nudged Waylon forward.

Waylon wiped the sweat from his brow before shaking his head. Then he poured out everything.

Katie couldn't believe what she was hearing.

Before she could ask any questions, the police arrived. They filled out an incident report before escorting Waylon away.

When he was gone, Dylan turned to her. "How are you after all this?"

She shrugged. "This is a lot to comprehend."

"I know. And I'm sorry." Dylan started to reach for her but stopped as if thinking better of it. "We need to get you out of here. I know you want to drive yourself home—"

"You can drive me." Katie frowned as if it pained

her to say the words. "I know I said I'd stay at my place tonight, but my stubbornness only goes so far. If it's okay with you, I'll sleep at your apartment again tonight."

Dylan's shoulders softened. "I'd feel a lot better if you did. Let's get going."

They went back to the office to grab their things before heading out.

Katie's thoughts raced as she and Dylan climbed into his SUV—or Maddox's, it appeared. Dylan remained on guard as he glanced around the dark parking lot.

She wanted to pretend she wasn't scared. But she was.

There was no denying that.

She expected Dylan to put the SUV into Drive and pull away.

Instead, he turned to her. "I have a few other updates."

He proceeded to tell her what Stiles had shared with him, as well as about the moonshine Brandon and Titus had found at Kingston's property.

"What?" Katie's voice came out breathless. "That's what all of this is about? You think Kingston is stealing *empty* containers—ones not full of acetone —and he's doing that so he can use them to store moonshine?"

Dylan offered a half shrug. "That's how it appears."

"And how do Donovan and Kingston know each other?" She let her head fall back against the headrest as thoughts pummeled her.

"Maybe he's selling moonshine to Donovan? I'm not sure yet. But there's one more thing."

"Don't keep me in suspense."

"The guys at Blackout found an address affiliated with New Life Enterprises."

Katie's breath caught. "They did? Where?"

"It's outside of Charlotte."

"We've got to go there."

He raised his hands as if to slow her thoughts. "I'm not sure that's a good idea."

"We can't go to the police yet. We don't have any proof. They won't take us seriously."

"So, what are you suggesting?"

"I just want to drive out there," Katie said. "Check it out. Maybe take some pictures. And if we discover this really is a lead worth looking into, *then* we can turn it over to the police."

"And that's it?" Dylan stared at her as if waiting for more.

"That's it. I know my capabilities. I know I'm not strong enough to take on a group of Donovan's men. But if they're doing something illegal, then we need to stop them. I just can't turn a blind eye toward what they're doing—especially if other people are suffering because of their greed."

Dylan seemed to consider her argument a moment before nodding. "I figured you were going to say that. That's why I almost didn't tell you. But you deserve to know."

Gratitude filled her. She *was* thankful that he didn't leave her out of the loop. She could see where doing so would have been tempting—and an easy way to keep her safe.

At least, he respected her enough to share that much.

"So, you'll go check it out with me?" She held her breath as she waited for his answer.

"Yes. But, first, let's go back to the apartment and change. You need something you can run in, that will blend in with the shadows."

Katie's heart skipped a beat.

Maybe this was the information she'd been looking for.

Maybe she'd figure out what Donovan was really up to and be able to stop the man for good.

MAYBE DYLAN SHOULDN'T HAVE SHARED that update with Katie.

But he'd meant his words when he'd said he couldn't keep the news from her either. She'd lost her career because of Donovan Sullivan. Besides, this was about more than her job.

If Katie's suspicions were correct, the man was trafficking innocent human beings.

Dylan understood her reasoning for not calling the police yet. Right now, the two of them were just going on a hunch. They'd only learned about this organization and the address associated with it because Katie had broken into Donovan's office.

They couldn't exactly admit that.

But Dylan still felt uneasy as he changed his clothes in his apartment.

He'd already told Maddox what was going on. Maddox would stay with Connie, just to be on the safe side.

Dylan stepped from his bedroom and into the hallway at the same time as Katie. He sucked in a breath at the sight of her.

She wore black jeans and a black sweatshirt along with sneakers. Her hair was pulled into a ponytail, and all her jewelry was gone.

Dylan cleared his throat, trying to push aside his attraction and focus on the mission at hand. "Are you sure you're ready for this?"

Katie stared at him, a stubborn look in her gaze. She finally nodded. "I am."

"What's going on?" Connie stepped out of the bathroom, her hair wet from her shower.

Katie gave her the update on everything— including the discovery on Kingston's property.

Connie adamantly shook her head, denial flashing in her gaze. "It's not moonshine."

"My colleagues found all the equipment," Dylan explained. "Kingston must have just been stealing empty containers to store his alcohol. Maybe he was never stealing acetone at all."

"There was *something* in those containers." Connie raised her chin. "I'm sure of it. If the containers had been empty, those boxes would have been lighter. He wouldn't have struggled with them."

Dylan looked at Katie. Her frown reflected his own feelings on this matter.

He'd hoped to put the incident with Kingston behind them for now.

By all appearances, he was illegally making and selling alcohol. That needed to be dealt with. But they had more pressing matters at hand right now.

"Maybe tomorrow we'll ask more questions," Katie said. "Right now, we have another lead we need to chase."

Connie crossed her arms as if unconvinced Dylan's words were the truth. But she didn't say anything.

Dylan glanced at his watch. It was already ten o'clock. At least, they'd have the cover of darkness to help conceal them on their stakeout.

But as they left, Dylan knew they might need more than that.

———

Anxiety gripped Katie as they got closer to the location.

There was nothing else around them right now—only miles and miles of forest and farmland.

She'd looked up the details of the property and had discovered it included a warehouse. The building had been abandoned for the last ten years. Then only six months ago, New Life Enterprises had bought the place.

Six months ago . . . that was around the time Katie had been fired.

Around the time she'd discovered the missing women who were vaguely affiliated with Donovan.

Could this be the piece of information she was looking for?

The company didn't have an online footprint. They didn't have a website. Didn't post anything on social media. It was as if they existed only on paper. They seemed to be purposefully veiled. Secretive.

What kind of company didn't need to market their products?

A mile from the address, Dylan pulled to a stop on the side of the road and put the SUV in Park.

He turned toward her, his gaze concerned as it met hers. "We're going to have to walk from here."

Katie nodded, wary of the zing she felt race through her blood when Dylan looked at her like that. He may have deceived her about who he really was. But his feelings hadn't been an act, had they?

She didn't have time to think about that right now. She swallowed hard as she shifted her thoughts.

"I expected we'd have to go in by foot," she murmured.

That didn't stop the tremble from raking through her as she stepped into the cool nighttime air.

She and Dylan walked silently through the trees at the edge of the road, trying to remain out of sight. Finally, they reached the end of a private drive.

A metal-sided warehouse surrounded by a barbed wire fence came into view a quarter mile away. A few dim lights were scattered outside the main entrance. A couple more shone around the property.

Dylan glanced around before nodding to a spot on the other side of the warehouse. "We need to go to that hill. It will give us a good vantage point to see what's going on."

Dylan's reasoning made sense, and he clearly had experience in these kinds of situations, so Katie didn't question him.

Quietly, they walked to the spot and then perched behind some trees to stay out of sight.

Katie got a better look at the warehouse. The whole place looked empty, like no one was there. No light leaked from the windows. No cars were parked nearby. Weeds grew in the gravel drive.

What if she and Dylan had come all the way out here for nothing? What if this lead was false?

Katie knew it was a possibility. Just because New

Life Enterprises had been imprinted on Donovan's calendar didn't mean it would lead to anything.

But she and Dylan had to at least give this a shot.

Speaking of his calendar . . . she pulled up the photo she'd taken of it on her phone.

"What is it?" Dylan asked.

"Just a hunch." She enlarged the image, focusing on his schedule for today.

At twelve, he was scheduled for yoga.

"Yoga? I can't see Donovan doing yoga," she muttered.

"It looks like he had another class scheduled two weeks ago, on a different day of the week." Dylan pointed at another notation on the calendar.

"That seems odd, doesn't it?"

He glanced at his watch. "Maybe that's not twelve noon but twelve midnight."

"What time is it now?"

"Two minutes till twelve."

Had Donovan disguised his meetings as exercise classes so no one would be suspicious?

Her breath caught at the thought.

She straightened when she spotted a large truck coming up the drive a minute later.

A box truck.

She and Dylan exchanged a quick look.

The driver stopped at the gate, and someone stepped out of the cab to unlock the chain.

Katie grabbed Dylan's arm as they watched.

This was it.

The moment Katie and Dylan would find out if they would get some answers or not.

THIRTY-NINE

DYLAN MOTIONED for Katie to stay in place as they watched the truck pull through the gate toward the warehouse.

The driver didn't back into the delivery bay. Instead, he parked in the empty lot, parallel to the building.

Dylan's gut told him that something unsavory was happening here. Most shipments didn't come in the middle of the night—not when things were on the up and up.

His eyes remained glued to the scene as two men with guns in their hands climbed from the cab and walked to the back of the vehicle. They opened the doors and motioned to someone inside.

The next instant, people began flooding out.

A lot of people.

At least thirty.

They must have been crammed in that space like sardines.

Anger shot up Dylan's spine.

People.

People were the commodity here.

"This is just what I suspected," Katie whispered. "Donovan is involved in human trafficking."

Dylan clenched his jaw.

The way these folks were being ushered into the building reminded Dylan of cows headed to slaughter.

Two more armed guards emerged from the back, yelling and shoving the people forward.

Dylan squeezed his fists tighter. It took every bit of his self-control not to launch from his position and confront the guards. That would be foolish. There were at least four armed guards with military-grade weapons.

It was too risky for Dylan to confront them alone.

If they started shooting, too many people could get hurt.

"This makes me sick to my stomach," Katie whispered before snapping several pictures with her phone. "This is the proof I need. I'm going to take Donovan down, one way or another."

"We need to get the police out here." Dylan

grabbed his phone. "We have to stop this before these people are transported somewhere else."

But before he could dial, a stick cracked behind him.

———

Katie felt her spine go ramrod straight.

"Don't try anything or I'll shoot," a deep voice said.

The hairs on the back of her neck stood on end.

The four men were still in sight near the warehouse.

Where had this guy even come from?

Slowly, she and Dylan raised their hands as they turned around.

A man with a semiautomatic rifle stood over them, gun pointed at Katie's chest.

Katie had never seen the thirty-something man before. He wore all black and talked as if he'd been a soldier at one time.

How had he even known she and Dylan were here?

"You shouldn't have come here," the man growled, keeping his gun aimed at Katie.

"Look, man, we were just exploring the woods when—" Dylan started.

"Save it. Stand up and walk. Both of you."

Dylan glanced at Katie and nodded. Slowly, they both rose from the ground. The man pointed down the hill toward the warehouse.

"Walk," he ordered. "Make any sudden moves, and I'll shoot. Don't test me."

As Dylan and Katie stepped forward, the man raised his radio to his lips. "Looks like we have two more people to add to the mix. We'll get good money for them. In the meantime, pack everyone else back up. It's not safe for us to stay here."

Fury burned in Katie's blood.

These men were heartless. They didn't care about anything except money and how they could benefit from the misfortune of others.

Now that these guys knew they'd been discovered, they would flee with these innocent people.

What if it was too late to stop them by the time backup got here?

If Katie and Dylan got into that truck with these people, there was a good chance no one would ever see them again. Katie knew how these types of criminals worked. They'd stop at nothing to get what they wanted.

"You guys thought you were so clever, parking so far away," the man said. "We have sensors that alert us if anyone comes within fifty feet of the property.

We knew the moment you two stepped near the fence."

"You guys are clearly the clever ones," Dylan muttered.

"Don't think I don't know who you are. Dylan Granger, former Navy SEAL. Katie Logan, disgraced reporter. You both should have just left well enough alone."

Katie felt certain Dylan had a gun with him. But if he reached for it, this guy might pull the trigger. It was too risky.

But they couldn't just let these traffickers get away with this either. They couldn't make it easy on them.

Katie nearly stumbled on a rock, but Dylan caught her elbow.

As he did, the man lunged toward Dylan as if he feared Dylan would make a move.

In one swift action, Dylan turned. With one hand, he shoved the man's gun aside. With the other, he rammed his fist into the man's jaw.

The guard reeled back, his gun tumbling to the ground and landing on a rock below them.

Dylan didn't give the man a chance to retrieve it.

Instead, he jammed his shoulder into the man's stomach.

Katie scrambled toward the gun and grasped the

weapon in her hands. She raised it, trying to figure out where to aim.

The men were all over the place as fists flew and grunts escaped.

Her lungs tightened.

She didn't want to pull the trigger and accidentally hurt Dylan.

The idea of doing that . . . it felt devastating.

Dear God . . . what should I do?

If she fired, that would alert the other gunmen. They'd have more guards to fend off.

Finally, Dylan pinned the man on the rocky ground. Blood ran from the guy's nose, and his eye already looked swollen.

He was down for the count.

Katie pointed the gun at him just in case he got any ideas. "Don't make a move or I'll shoot."

"But—"

"Save it." Katie used the man's exact words from earlier.

It gave her immense pleasure to throw them back in his face.

But her pleasure only lasted a moment.

She and Dylan were a long way from finding any resolution right now.

KATIE KEPT the gun aimed on the man who'd nearly taken them out.

"We don't have time to wait for anyone else to get here." Dylan pulled himself up straight as he glanced at the guard beside him. "Those men are loading people back up, and they're going to take them away. We won't have time to get back to the SUV and follow. Besides, they're expecting this guy to bring us down there to join them."

"What do you want to do?" Katie's heart thrummed with anticipation. His words were true. How they responded right now could determine the fate of these people's lives.

"While I secure this guy, you call the police."

Dylan pulled zip ties from his pocket and began binding the man's feet and hands together. Then he ripped a piece off the bottom of his T-shirt and tied it around the man's mouth to gag him.

As he worked, Katie dialed 911 and asked for immediate help.

When Dylan finished, he grabbed the man's radio and an extra gun from his waist and handed them to Katie. Then he stood, took the rifle back from Katie, and looked toward the warehouse.

"I'm going to go slow them down," Dylan muttered. "These guys know we're out here. They're on guard right now. Follow me and stay close."

Katie sucked in a deep breath as adrenaline pumped through her. "You think it'll be okay if we leave this guy here?"

They both glanced back at the man. He lay on the ground, struggling against his binds. But he wasn't going anywhere.

"He'll be fine for a few minutes," Dylan said.

When they neared the warehouse, Dylan motioned for her to hide behind a tree.

They were closer now. Close enough to make out the victims' faces. To hear murmuring. To see the panic in people's eyes.

Fear laced the air, nearly cracking it with tension.

Dylan perched behind another tree with the rifle.

Katie stared at him, wondering exactly what he was planning. "Dylan?"

Her heart thumped in her ears as she stared at him.

This man had truly been a warrior, hadn't he? He'd fought for other people. Put his own safety on the line. Had done whatever was necessary to help others.

She'd initially seen him as a bookworm. He was anything but. Yet another part of him was so gentle and compassionate.

"Did I mention I was a sharpshooter in my past life as a Navy SEAL?"

"What?" Her voice came out wispy. "No, you didn't mention that fact."

"I would have told you earlier, but you weren't exactly talking to me."

She couldn't argue that point.

Dylan raised the rifle to his shoulder as he set up his target.

Katie held her breath.

Was he going to shoot one of the guards? Would the men then turn around in retaliation and shoot the people they held captive? A moment of panic raced through her.

She was used to taking down people with words. With facts.

Not with weapons.

Dylan pulled the trigger, and a bullet whizzed

through the air.

A hissing sound followed.

The truck suddenly shifted, leaning to one side.

Dylan had hit one of their tires, Katie realized.

Brilliant.

Then he took out another one.

The men scrambled to take cover.

"This should buy us some time." Dylan glanced back at her. "We just have to make sure these guys don't hurt anyone in the meantime. I need you to stay here and act as a lookout."

Alarm raced through her. "What are you going to do?"

"I'm going to make an opening in that fence so I can get closer."

"Dylan . . ." Her throat swelled with emotions.

"You know how to use that gun if you need to?"

She nodded, her throat tight. "Yes, I've taken lessons."

"Good."

"Bernard, what's going on out there?" a voice crackled over the radio.

Katie and Dylan glanced at each other, each sharing the same concerned expression.

"This means we're out of time," Dylan said. "They're going to realize he's missing."

She nodded again.

Dylan's gaze locked with hers. "I need you to trust me, okay? I can't afford any distractions. I need to know that you're safe. Promise me you'll stay here. Please."

Katie stared at him another moment before letting out a long breath. "Okay. I promise."

Then she watched as Dylan darted toward the fence . . . and toward danger.

———

Dylan tucked the gun under his arm before using some clippers he'd brought in his backpack to sever the chain-link fence. Once he had an opening, he climbed through and ran until he reached the warehouse and ducked behind the corner.

He couldn't make himself an easy target.

Since there was only one of him and four other guys were still a threat, he'd have to be very careful.

Dylan paused and raised his rifle again.

As panic set in, two men began ushering people toward the warehouse. Their truck was now useless.

The remaining guards began shooting in his direction.

It would be a harder shot, but he could do it.

When he had the first man in his sights, he pulled the trigger.

The bullet hit the man's gun, and the weapon flew from his hand.

Shouts sounded as the other guards began scrambling. People screamed.

Chaos ensued.

The two men who had been shooting at him kept their weapons ready as they searched for Dylan.

Dylan ducked back and quickly glanced behind him to check on Katie.

He did a double take.

She was . . . gone.

Gone?

Had someone grabbed her? Had there been another security guard in the woods?

His heart thumped into his chest.

He glanced at the scene near the truck again.

That's when he spotted her.

Katie was with the people who'd been trafficked.

She was leading them toward the woods to safety while Dylan distracted the guards.

"Hey!" One of the men spotted her and lifted his weapon.

Wasting no time, Dylan raised his gun again.

He took the shot and hit the truck window. Glass shattered and cascaded down on the two men standing nearby.

One of the guards gasped, dropping his gun. The other opened his door and took cover.

Katie barely glanced back. Instead, she kept leading people toward the woods.

The remaining guards scrambled to locate Dylan.

A bullet flew past him. Then another. And another.

He remained behind the building, his heart pounding into his chest.

He didn't want to hurt anyone—not unless he had to.

And that appeared to be the case right now.

He raised his weapon. Got one of the men in his sights. His fingers lingered near the trigger.

But before he could fire, spotlights illuminated the parking lot, followed by shouts of, "Police!"

Dylan glanced beyond the fence and saw that help had arrived.

Several officers had everyone surrounded.

The remaining guards slowly lowered their guns to the ground before raising their hands.

Dylan lowered his gun also, a breath of relief rushing from his lungs.

It appeared this was all over.

For now, at least.

WHEN THE POLICE finished questioning her, Katie wandered away from the cop who'd taken her statement and glanced around. Three hours had passed since the cops had shown up.

Ten police cars surrounded the property along with multiple ambulances. Two other members of Blackout were here as well—Brandon and a younger man named Titus.

It appeared most of the victims were refugees from Asia who'd been lured to the United States with promises of jobs and housing. Most were single women, and several were teens.

From what Katie understood after talking to some of them, they'd been placed in the back of this truck when they'd arrived in the States six months ago and had been transported from location to location doing odd jobs.

Most of them were malnourished. Several were sick.

Some had gone missing along the way.

Katie hoped that with some leads, the cops would be able to track down each and every person.

She really hoped that many arrests would be made tonight and many more in the future.

There were clearly more people involved in this than just the men who'd transported these people.

People like Donovan.

She paced the parking lot until she found Dylan leaning against the back of a police cruiser as he talked to a cop.

He was okay. Thank God, he was okay.

Katie had known it would be risky to leave the spot where Dylan had left her.

But she'd seen the panic on those people's faces, and she'd known she had to help.

However, she wasn't sure how Dylan would react to her now.

She paused in front of him and waited for the cop to finish asking questions. Finally, the officer closed his notebook and walked away.

Then she told Dylan, "Good job. That was some fancy shooting you did back there."

"I'm glad my skills came in handy," he murmured. "I guess I should tell you good job also. I want to be mad, but I can't be."

His big eyes glimmered with . . . something.

Affection? Relief?

Katie wasn't sure.

Her throat tightened, though. She wanted to let down her guard. To tell Dylan that all was forgiven.

But would that be wise?

She wanted to throw logic out the window.

But how could she?

Dylan had deceived her. Maybe that alone wasn't inexcusable. She believed in forgiveness. What was more difficult was forgetting and moving forward.

"Who were those guards?" Katie asked.

"I know at least two of them were Dagger agents. Wherever trouble is, that's where they seem to be."

"Dagger?"

"They're like Blackout, only they have no ethics."

Katie's eyes widened. "If that's the case, why isn't the agency shut down?"

His gaze darkened. "They were once, but they reassembled. I'm sure these guys will deny it. They'll say they were working off the books. That's the way they operate."

She frowned as she glanced at an ambulance in

the distance with one of the men inside. "It looks like they all survived . . ."

"I shot strategically. I wanted to stop them, not kill them."

Katie could definitely appreciate that about him. These men might be evil, but she was more comfortable with the judicial system handling them.

"Are the police going to have to take you in?" she asked.

Dylan shook his head. "I gave my statement and promised to stick around town if they have more questions. My bullets didn't actually hit anyone."

No doubt, he planned it that way.

"It sounds like I'm free to go whenever I want," Dylan said.

"That's good." Katie stared up at him, still unsure what to say.

And she was hardly ever unsure of herself.

She wanted so badly to trust him. But fear stopped her from doing so.

She'd trusted her cameraman—a guy named Luke Simpkins. He was the only person she'd confided in about what she'd discovered.

She found out later that he was the one who'd told Donovan what she was doing. The man had practically been a spy for Donovan the whole time.

After Katie was fired, Luke left the network. Katie

had a feeling he'd been paid well for the information he offered—paid well enough that he no longer had to work.

"Dylan . . ." Katie licked her lips, not sure what words would leave her mouth.

"Yes?" Hope flickered in his gaze.

"I just wanted to let you know—"

"Good work, you two," someone interrupted.

She glanced up and saw Detective Morris there.

"All these people will be taken to shelters tonight," he continued. "They'll have food and medical care. A safe place to sleep. I'm glad you called us when you did. Maybe a little earlier next time."

"Hopefully, there won't be a next time." Dylan crossed his arms.

"Have you been able to track down Donovan Sullivan yet?" Katie rushed, anxious to know if the man had been caught.

The case now seemed like a slam dunk.

This atrocity had happened on his property, with his company, and no doubt these were men he'd hired.

Morris rubbed his jaw, almost as if covering a frown. "Mr. Sullivan did purchase this property, and he plans to do something with it one day. He wants to start a company called New Life Enterprises that will help those down on their luck find jobs and housing. But Mr. Sullivan said he hasn't put anything into action yet—other than registering the business name. He's still in the planning stages."

"And . . ." Katie waited for him to continue, praying there was a "but" in there.

She didn't buy Donovan's explanation.

The man probably wanted to use his supposed company as a cover for more human trafficking operations.

"We believe someone else thought this property was abandoned and was using the area for nefarious purposes," Morris finally finished.

"You can't believe that." Dylan's hands went to his hips.

Morris offered a half shrug. "We'll continue to look into it, of course. We'll show Mr. Sullivan's picture to a few people and see if they recognize him. See if there's any kind of paper trail."

"And you'll look into who these guys are working for?" Katie interjected, her confidence in this investigation instantly nosediving.

"Of course." Morris almost seemed to answer that a little too quickly.

Anger shot up her spine, and Katie decided to get right to the point. "Mr. Sullivan is *not* telling the truth. Please don't tell me you're falling for his lies."

Morris's eyes narrowed as he coldly assessed her. "You're not exactly objective in this case, are you, Ms. Logan? The man *did* get you fired. It's normal that you'd want some retaliation."

His words contained a biting sting of accusation.

Katie bit her tongue before she said something she'd regret. Morris clearly thought she had a vendetta against Donovan.

In truth, all she wanted was justice.

The detective couldn't believe all those excuses Donovan had given him.

Yet that seemed to be the case.

"That question is out of line." Anger simmered beneath Dylan's even tones.

"Of course, we'll investigate every angle." Morris shifted, his silent accusations fading. "But right now, what's happening here appears to be a separate operation from Mr. Sullivan."

Katie could *not* let Donovan get away with this again. But that's exactly what it seemed was going to happen.

Donovan would use his influence and money to get away with this. How many more people would be hurt in the process?

As Morris walked away, Dylan pressed his hand on her shoulder. "We'll get this guy one way or another."

Her stomach knotted with tension as she realized she'd just come up against what felt like an insurmountable wall. "I hate people who think they're untouchable."

"No one is untouchable."

She glanced back at the scene, at the officers who handed water to the people who'd been in the truck. At the paramedics who treated the injured men. At the flashing lights and crime-scene tape.

She shook her head as she tried to process everything. "There's more to all that's been happening, in addition to Donovan Sullivan. I'm sure of it."

Dylan's jaw visibly tightened. "What do you mean?"

"Someone hired some thugs to silence me. This person even used Dean Sears to further his plan."

"Most likely, this person hired Dagger—and blackmailed Waylon."

"This operation is part of what I researched before I got fired. But I backed off and stayed quiet, deciding to keep my investigation under wraps. Nothing I did should have triggered them to come after me."

"Okay . . ."

"So that goes back to Kingston again. I did a couple of stakeouts by his house. I also called his secretary and pretended to be a magazine reporter who wanted to feature him. We went through his schedule trying to find a good time to schedule his interview. All the while, I took note of times he wasn't available. There's a chance he could have discovered what I was doing."

"You think he would do all of that to you over moonshine?"

She shrugged. "I don't know."

"What about when we were chased from Donovan's party? That couldn't have been Kingston. He wasn't there."

"But his parents were . . ." She shrugged again and let out a long breath. "I don't know. If Kingston and Donovan are connected, then Kingston could have heard I was there."

Dylan nodded slowly. "You may be right."

"I just don't feel like this is the end of it."

Dylan's phone rang, interrupting their conversation. "It's Maddox. Let me make sure everything is okay."

Katie listened to Dylan's side of the conversation, trying to pick up on what was being said.

"What?" Dylan's eyebrows shot up. "Are you sure?"

Tension filled Katie again.

Something else was wrong, wasn't it?

A moment later, Dylan lowered his phone and

glanced at her with trepidation in his gaze. "Connie's gone."

"What?" Katie squeaked.

"Maddox just went to her room to give her the update on the situation. When she didn't answer, he cracked the door open, and her bedroom was empty. It looks like she snuck out during the middle of the night."

"But her car's not even at the apartment complex . . ."

"He checked the security footage. It looks like she called for a driver. Now we just need to figure out where she went."

———

Dylan saw the alarm spread across Katie's face as he told her about Connie.

"Do you really think she snuck out?" Katie's voice nearly sounded breathless as she stared up at him. "What if someone grabbed her?"

"Maddox would have heard if someone took her."

"But wouldn't he have heard if she snuck out?"

Dylan shrugged. "Not if she was quiet. Let's just assume right now she did sneak out. Do you have any idea where she would have gone?"

Katie's eyes traveled back and forth in thought. "The only thing I can think of is that she went to find out more dirt on Kingston. This whole time, Connie has claimed he was up to something bigger than moonshine. What if she went to confront him herself?"

Dylan's heart pounded in his ears. "Would she do something like that?"

"I want to say no, but I can tell the guy gets under her skin—kind of like Donovan gets under my skin. Maybe Connie is afraid Kingston will walk away scot-free."

Dylan narrowed his eyes as he tried to follow her line of reasoning. "But what would she do? Would she confront him?"

Katie pressed her lips together a moment before shaking her head. "I don't think so. She hates conflict. But she may have gone to find answers. Proof."

His mind raced through various possibilities before he finally asked, "Do you think she went back to that farm we discovered?"

"I'd say that's a good guess. Wait. That app I have!" Katie pulled out her phone and tapped a few things. "I almost forgot. I can check that for her location."

"Where does it say she is now?" Dylan asked.

Katie typed a few things before holding her phone up as if trying to get better reception. A moment later, her eyes lit.

The excitement quickly morphed into fear as she turned back to Dylan. "We were right. She went back to that farm we told her about. She must have been able to figure out the location based on what we described."

Dylan's eyes widened. "If Connie went there, then there's a good chance she's in trouble. We need to get there."

"Let's go." Katie stepped toward the woods leading to their SUV.

Dylan didn't argue as he followed behind.

KATIE'S MIND RACED.

How could Connie do this?

But Katie knew.

She and Connie, in some ways, were cut from the same cloth. While Connie was shy and more insecure, she still had a driving need for justice.

That's why her cousin had decided to take things into her own hands.

Maybe Katie should have listened when Connie insisted Kingston was up to something else. But it was too late to change that now.

"We're going to find her." Dylan's deep, soothing voice pulled Katie from her rash of fearful thoughts.

"I just hope she's okay. Stiles said his best friend saw Donovan and Kingston meeting . . . do you think they're in this together? Maybe the moonshine and trafficking are somehow a joint venture."

"It's a possibility."

Katie's heart hammered her chest as they headed down the road. Asheville was still thirty minutes away, and right now it felt as if they'd never get there.

She just needed to know that Connie was safe.

She'd tried to both call and text her cousin, but it was almost as if Connie's phone had been disabled. It only showed the last location where she'd been.

By the time they reached Asheville, the sun peeked out over the mountaintops. In some ways, the daylight would make it easier. In other ways, it could expose them.

Dylan followed the road toward the farm and parked in the same area as before. Then the two of them started hiking through the woods.

But they'd have to be careful. They couldn't alert anyone to the fact they were coming.

As they got closer to the farm, Katie slowed her steps and braced herself for whatever she was about to find.

————

Dylan didn't like the scenarios running through his head. He prayed Connie was okay and that this was a misunderstanding. Yet, he knew that probably wasn't the case.

As he and Katie got closer, he spotted several vehicles outside the barn.

Including Kingston's red truck.

He and Katie lingered at the edge of the woods to get a feel for the situation before creeping closer.

Dylan had already counted four men on the scene. Most of them had guns.

If Connie was here, he and Katie would definitely need backup.

He texted his team again.

Brandon texted back that they were already on their way and had picked up Maddox.

"What's our next move?" Katie whispered as she crouched behind a bush.

"Right now, we're gathering info." Dylan nodded at the scene in front of them. "Let's move around the perimeter of the area for a better look."

As they reached the back side of the barn, Katie gasped.

"That's Connie's car," she whispered, pointing to an old blue sedan that had been stashed between some trees in the distance. "She must have had her driver drop her off at her car—probably after she bought enough gas to make it to a station."

Connie appeared to be just as resourceful as her cousin.

He hoped that didn't prove to be fatal.

Just then, a cry came from inside the barn.

Katie grasped his arm. "It's her. Connie. I'm certain of it. It sounds like she's in trouble."

Dylan wasn't sure he could wait for backup to arrive. It sounded like Connie's life was in danger.

When he saw two men leaving the barn, Dylan knew this was his opportunity to make a move.

He motioned for Katie to follow behind him as he drew his gun.

Then they darted toward the back of the building.

CHAPTER
FORTY-THREE

KATIE COULD HARDLY BREATHE AS she followed Dylan toward the barn.

Every time she heard Connie cry out, her heart plummeted.

What were these men doing to her cousin inside this barn?

Whatever it was, Katie needed to put an end to it before her cousin was seriously hurt.

Dylan took her hand as they darted through a door into the back of the building. They ducked out of sight behind some hay bales.

As Katie peered over one, she spotted Connie.

Her cousin sat in an old wooden chair in the middle of the barn, arms bound behind her, a rope tied around her midsection. A man with a gun paced in front of her, and another man stood near the front door.

"You should have never come here," the man with the gun said.

"I told you. I just got lost." Connie's voice cracked.

"We know who you are. You work for Baylor Beauty."

"So do a lot of people in this area. That doesn't mean I'm here trying to do anything."

"Even if you weren't, it's too late," the man growled. "You know too much, and now we have to figure out a way to keep you quiet."

"I won't tell anybody. I promise." Connie's voice shifted from fearful to downright desperate.

"Sorry, that's not going to work. Promises are cheap."

Connie stared at the man. "What are you going to do with me?"

"That's for Kingston to decide."

Dylan and Katie exchanged a glance. Kingston Baylor was *definitely* involved in this.

"I think the easiest way to handle this would just be with a bullet," the gunman grumbled. "It's fast and painless, with fairly easy cleanup. We can dump your body deep into these woods, and it will be months before anyone finds you. If at all."

"What makes you think that?" Connie's voice trembled. "I have people who love me. They'll look for me."

"Then maybe we'll take care of them too."

Connie gasped. "No . . ."

"Why are you looking at me like I'm the bad guy? This is all your fault."

"What are you even doing here that's so important? That's so much of a secret?"

"Wouldn't you like to know?" The man paused in front of Connie and mocked her curious expression.

"I'm going to die anyway, so it doesn't matter. Right?"

He shook his head, almost as if he pitied her. "We have a plan. No one is going to stop us."

"What kind of plan?"

"A plan that's going to change this place as we know it."

Katie's heart beat harder. This was bigger than she'd anticipated. What did he mean by "this place"?

She glanced beside her.

Several plastic containers full of clear liquid were stacked in crates there.

Moonshine. The moonshine the Blackout team hadn't found last time.

Or was it really moonshine?

Moonshine wasn't nearly high-stakes enough for the kind of danger that saturated the air.

Carefully, she unscrewed the top of one and took a sniff.

The scent nearly took her breath away.

This wasn't alcohol.

It was definitely acetone.

Connie had been right all along.

The moonshine must have just been a cover in case anyone asked any questions.

The man's phone rang, and he muttered a few things into it.

Then he turned back to Connie with a smirk. "I just got permission to finish this job."

With those words, he stepped back and aimed his gun directly at Connie's forehead.

———

If Dylan was going to act, he had to do it now.

He stepped from behind the hay bale and aimed his gun at the man. "Put your weapon down."

The man's eyes widened, and he swerved his gun toward Dylan.

Before the man could pull the trigger, Dylan fired.

The bullet hit the man's shoulder, and he stumbled backward to the ground. The gun skittered from his hand.

Dylan had avoided having his bullets hit anyone at the last scene. But, right now, it was shoot them or they were going to shoot Connie. Dylan couldn't let that happen.

The gunman near the door rushed toward Dylan.

Dylan already had the man in his sights. Dylan pulled the trigger again, and the second man fell to the ground.

But there were more men outside.

Dylan and Katie had to rescue Connie and then run.

"Come on!" Dylan said.

He and Katie took off toward Connie. As they did, Dylan withdrew his pocketknife. As soon as they reached Connie, he began sawing the ropes binding her.

"You guys . . . you came." Connie's voice cracked as tears poured from her eyes.

"We don't have much time." Dylan still worked the thick rope. "We need to get out of here."

"I'm so sorry to bring you guys into this."

"It's okay," Dylan muttered. "We'll talk later. Right now, we just need to move."

The rope broke free from around her, and Connie

stood. Katie took her arm and pulled her toward the back exit.

But just as they reached the door, a shadow fell over them from behind, followed by a click.

"Stop right there if you know what's best for you."

Dylan froze, wanting to turn and pull his trigger again.

But he knew they were outnumbered.

He glanced back and spotted Kingston standing there, his pistol aimed at them. Two men flanked him, one at either side.

"Put your gun down," Kingston ordered.

"Don't hurt anyone." Dylan set his gun down slowly and then stepped forward, placing himself in front of the two women.

He wished he could tell them to run, but he knew any movement would be risky. Instead, he inched closer to the hay bales, indicating for the women to stay behind him. At least the bales would offer a small measure of protection.

"You guys. I should have known it was only a matter of time until you showed up here." Kingston paced closer before pausing in front of him. "You're going to wish that you didn't."

"You know who we are?" Katie asked.

"I didn't—not until about an hour ago when I got the update."

"You mean, the update on what happened at the warehouse?" Katie continued.

"Maybe. What's it to you?"

"I'm just trying to put pieces together," Katie said.

"I guess you always try to do that. You and your cousin too." He glared at Connie. "Someone told me she was asking questions at work. I had my guys try to scare her off, but it didn't work. Then she disappeared. Thankfully, she showed up here and made our job easier."

A small cry escaped from Connie.

"Who told you what happened at the warehouse?" With that admission, Kingston was clearly connected with Donovan Sullivan, Dylan mused.

"I have people."

"What are you and Donovan up to?" Katie demanded.

"Wouldn't you like to know?" Kingston smirked.

"Human trafficking." Katie raised her chin. "I know that much. I just don't know how you're connected with this. Or how moonshine could be connected."

His smirk widened.

This wasn't about moonshine, was it?

That really wasn't a surprise.

"If you're going to kill us, why don't you tell us what's going on?" Dylan locked his gaze with Kingston's.

"Why should I tell you? To satisfy your curiosity?" Kingston's smirk quickly transformed into a frown. "You guys have just created more trouble for us. That's the last thing we want."

"I think you're already in enough trouble as it is," Dylan muttered.

Kingston's eyes narrowed. "It looks like I'm going to have to take care of this situation myself. And, by situation . . . I mean, you guys."

"It's too late. We have backup on the way. Whatever you have going on here will be uncovered."

"Not if there's no proof left." As Kingston raised his gun again, Dylan ducked to the side.

But Kingston didn't aim at Dylan. Or at Connie or Katie.

He aimed at a plastic container filled with liquid and pulled the trigger.

The bullet went through the plastic and liquid poured out, flooding the area.

That's when Dylan knew what Kingston had in mind. He was not only going to kill them—but he would get rid of any other proof of the operations that had been going on here.

He'd probably already moved most of his product out. What was left here was just collateral damage.

They were just collateral damage.

The liquid was flammable. Explosive.

A spark from a bullet could ignite it.

And that was exactly what Kingston had in mind.

"Don't do it!" Dylan took a step back, inching closer to the ladies in a futile effort to protect them.

The next instant, Kingston pulled a Zippo lighter out of his pocket, flicked it on, and tossed it into the liquid.

Instantly, flames erupted.

Dylan's breath caught.

They had to get out of here.

Now.

This old barn would go up in mere minutes.

"Run!" Dylan told the ladies.

Before he could follow them through the exit, Kingston rammed his fist into his jaw.

Dylan's head spun, but he quickly righted himself.

Flames whipped behind him.

At least Katie and Connie had gotten out.

But as he faced off with Kingston, he realized this battle wasn't over yet.

Not even close.

KATIE HAD no choice but to leave with Connie. She couldn't let her cousin get hurt.

She tucked Connie behind a tree in the woods before she started back toward the barn to help Dylan.

She didn't know exactly what she could do. But she couldn't leave Dylan by himself.

The whole barn could go up in flames at any moment. And if Dylan was inside . . . there was no way he'd survive.

Katie glanced around, trying to figure out the best solution.

As her gaze stopped on an abandoned container sitting outside the barn, an idea formed in her mind.

It was risky, but it just might work.

She grabbed the container and ran with it to the

front of the barn. As she darted inside, she stopped in her tracks.

Kingston was closest to her, just as she'd thought.

Flames climbed the barn's side walls.

She swallowed hard, praying she was making the right choice.

Then she twisted off the container's lid and began dumping the liquid, leaving a trail behind her.

As she got closer to the flames, Katie knew exactly what would happen.

Again, she prayed this wouldn't backfire.

Then she doused the flames, connecting what was already burning to the flammable liquid she'd just poured.

The next instant, this side of the barn exploded with fire.

Blocking Kingston from exiting through the front door.

She heard a yell.

Her breath caught.

Was that Kingston?

Or was it Dylan?

———

Dylan saw Katie and wondered what she was doing.

Then flames erupted around Kingston.

She'd just added accelerant to the fire, hadn't she?

Kingston's sidekicks took off running out the back door, heading for safety.

But not Kingston.

Kingston took another swing at Dylan.

Dylan ducked. The motion caused Kingston to lose his balance, and he stepped backward into the inferno.

The next moment, fire licked at Kingston's pants. As the flames climbed, the blaze consumed the man.

Kingston shouted in pain then dived onto the floor and rolled in the hay.

Dylan glanced through the flames at Katie.

She nodded at him before running out the front door.

Dylan looked at Kingston one more time.

He was still fighting to put out the flames on his clothes.

Time was running out.

This whole place could collapse at any minute.

He couldn't just leave the man here.

With a sigh, Dylan grabbed an old horse blanket and threw it over Kingston.

The lack of oxygen killed the flames, though the man was still smoldering.

Then Dylan helped him to his feet and led him outside.

Just as they stepped out the back, fire consumed the whole barn.

Moments later, the police arrived.

This operation was shut down.

And Katie and Connie were safe.

CHAPTER
FORTY-FIVE

KATIE STOOD near the old farmhouse and watched as the police took several men into custody. As for Kingston . . . he was being taken to a medical facility—with a police transport.

Firefighters had put out the residual flames around the barn. By the time they'd arrived, the structure had burned to the ground. More containers had exploded, leaving no hope that anything inside could be salvaged.

Connie was being treated by a paramedic. She had some scrapes and a concussion, but she would be okay.

The rest of the Blackout team had arrived and helped sort out the details.

Maybe this really was all over.

Except for the fact that Donovan was still out there.

And that authorities still thought he was innocent.

Katie's stomach squeezed at the thought.

Kingston had said Marvin, Donovan's right-hand man, had set this up. He claimed Donovan had nothing to do with it. And the authorities seemed to believe him so far.

Would Kingston talk under pressure from the ATF? Would he admit to his connection with Donovan?

Even more, were the two of them up to something that had yet to be discovered? Kingston hadn't explained exactly what was going on or where the chemicals had been sent. Just what was Donovan planning to do with those people he'd trafficked into the country?

As the thoughts raced through her head, Dylan appeared beside her.

Katie pulled him into a hug.

When she'd thought she was going to lose him . . . she'd realized that seemed like the worst thing in the world that could happen.

She knew their relationship had started on rocky ground, but she wanted to see where it would lead.

She pulled away, but Dylan kept his arms tight around her as she gazed up at him.

"Do you believe me when I say I'm sorry?" His voice sounded hoarse with emotion.

Katie felt the moisture pool in her eyes as she nodded. "I do. I'm still not happy about it, but I understand. Besides, you've been a true lifesaver."

"What does all of this mean for you?" Dylan studied her face. "Everything we've discovered. Everything that's happened. The questions that remain unanswered."

She shrugged and let out a long breath. "It means I still need more evidence. I'm going to keep working on my story. And if I don't end up getting a job with another news station, then I'll publish this on my own. There are definitely options out there for me."

"So, you won't keep teaching?"

"I'll finish up my term, just as I promised. Then we'll see what happens from there."

"I have a feeling you're going to be getting a lot of offers—especially after you figure all this out." He smiled, that familiar admiration gleaming in his gaze.

"I guess we'll see."

Dylan's smile faded, and he shifted in front of her. "Katie, I know I've made a lot of mistakes. But the biggest mistake I could make would be letting you walk away. I didn't think I'd ever feel this way again.

I thought finding love was a once in a lifetime opportunity. But I was wrong."

Her heart thumped in her chest as she waited for him to continue.

"I know I've messed up. And I know I'll mess up more. That's a part of living, unfortunately. But I would love nothing more than if you'd give me another chance."

Katie didn't have to think about her answer. "Yes. Yes, I will."

A smile stretched across his face.

The next instant, he leaned toward her, and their lips met.

Everyone else around them disappeared, and, for a moment, it was just her and Dylan.

A man cleared his throat beside them.

They stepped back to see a man approaching them. ATF Agent Richard Florence.

"Sorry to interrupt, but I have more questions."

Katie let out a long breath. Maybe this man would help them since the detective had let his biases show.

Maybe she could convince this man that Donovan Sullivan was guilty.

She knew the truth. She might not be able to prove it.

But that didn't mean that she wasn't going to try.

EPILOGUE

DYLAN STROLLED along the sidewalk in front of the Daniel Oliver Building, holding Katie's hand in his as he gave her the tour of Blackout's Lantern Beach headquarters.

Two weeks had passed since the showdown in Charlotte and Asheville.

Kingston was still in the hospital, but he had been charged on several counts—including kidnapping and attempted murder.

Donovan Sullivan had been cleared of any wrong-doing, and Marvin Pearsall would most likely be going to prison for a long time.

The thought still infuriated Dylan. Donovan was clearly a part of this.

Marvin had taken the blame, however. He claimed he'd hired men to scare Katie off—by following her, trying to run her over in the parking lot, ramming her father's car. He was the one who'd blackmailed Dean Sears into unlocking the door so the gunman could get inside the lecture hall and who'd instructed Sears to leave the note with the knife on Katie's desk.

Dagger hadn't officially been associated with the hired guns. But Dylan knew the truth. Everything had been done off-books. That was how Dagger operated.

Joe Faulkner was also still out there. Even though Dylan knew the guy was involved, the cops would find no evidence he was associated with any of the crimes that had taken place. Faulkner was in the wind, but Dylan had no doubt he'd see the man again someday.

"This is lovely." Katie's voice pulled Dylan back to the present. "I don't know if I'd want to live here, though. I'm not sure I'd ever get any work done."

He glanced at the sandy island around them, including the Pamlico Sound that edged the property in the distance. "It is nice to be here. Between jobs, it's a good place to unwind."

"I can imagine it makes for a nice getaway."

Dylan paused and turned toward her. "I'm hoping you might want to come here and unwind with me sometime."

Katie looped her arms around his neck and grinned. "That is a *very* tempting offer. I think I might be able to squeeze that into my schedule from time to time."

"Only six more weeks until summer break at UC."

"They've agreed to let me come back on a part-time basis. That means, I can take the job with Syndical News."

Syndical was a national news network. Even though Donovan Sullivan was still a free man, Katie's coverage of the human trafficking operation had gained her favor with multiple network executives. Her earlier "indiscretions" appeared to have been forgotten.

"I'm really proud of you." Dylan dipped his head and gently pressed his lips to her forehead. "But I would have been proud whether you'd gotten the job or not."

Katie smiled, her face practically glowing as she looked up at him. "Thank you. That means a lot."

The two of them had talked every night and taken turns visiting each other on their time off. So far, it had worked out well.

Dylan knew Katie Logan was one special woman. He couldn't wait to see what the future held for them. He even thought Rachel would give her stamp of approval.

"One thing is still bothering me," Katie muttered, twisting her lips into a frown.

Dylan could see her thoughts turning. "What's that?"

She stepped back and let out a deep breath. "Kingston . . . when he was in the barn. He said something about 'a plan that's going to change this place as we know it.' What do you think he was referring to?"

"I have no idea." Dylan had thought about his words also. They were unsettling. But Kingston hadn't admitted to anything yet—not as far as Dylan knew.

"Do you think . . . do you think Donovan has more tricks up his sleeve? I mean, the police still haven't found the remaining containers of acetone. Connie is certain he took more than what we saw inside that barn, and his guys verified that. But they claim they don't know what happened to those containers."

"The FBI will keep looking until they find answers. I feel confident of that."

"I can't help but think those products are connected in some way to whatever Donovan was planning to do with those people he trafficked into the country," Katie said. "I know Marvin claims he brought them in with plans of making them work in a factory for a startup, but I don't buy that."

"The important thing is that they were rescued."

Katie nodded, but that frown still twisted her lips. "That is important. And it's important that we stopped these men before they could proceed. Whatever plans they had, they're no longer happening. Donovan lost all his little helpers."

"I suppose you're right."

Dylan rubbed her arms. "Anyway . . . let's not think about it right now. Right now, let's enjoy the moment."

"Probably a good idea."

Before they could talk anymore, Maddox strode from the building, a backpack strung across his shoulder as he headed toward them.

"Katie . . ." Maddox paused. "I heard you were here, and I was hoping I might run into you."

"Is that right?"

Maddox reached into his pack, pulled out a plastic bag stuffed full of something, and handed it to her.

She peered inside. "Beanies?"

"I was hoping you might give them to some of the people you rescued from the operation in Charlotte."

"That's a great idea." Katie smiled. "I'd be more than happy to."

She'd been working with them during her free time, trying to help in any way possible. Her dedication was admirable. She'd even called the man she'd spoken with in the Philippines and had been able to reconnect him with his daughter, Angel Tajan.

Maddox shrugged. "Dylan said you've stayed in touch with them."

"I have. I'm not sure what exactly will happen to them—if they'll be sent back to their home countries or not. But, for now, they're here. They need an advocate, so I thought, why not me?"

"I like that." Maddox adjusted his backpack again.

"Where are you heading?" Katie asked.

Maddox exchanged a look with Dylan before he said, "We've got a lead on some land we think is being used for nefarious purposes. I'm going to see what I can find out."

"Nefarious purposes?" Katie raised an eyebrow. "I'm intrigued. Sounds like an interesting story is waiting to be uncovered."

Maddox chuckled, the sound deep and rumbling as he shook his head. "You didn't hear that from me."

Dylan and Katie watched as he walked away, and then Dylan took Katie's hands in his.

"How about if I show you the ocean?" he murmured.

"I'll go anywhere with you, Dylan Granger."

"Anywhere?" He raised his eyebrows. "You mean that?"

"One hundred percent."

A grin stretched across his face. "I'm glad to hear that because I have some ideas in mind . . ."

"Then by all means . . . lead the way."

"You got it. I know the perfect place to start." Instead of heading toward the beach, Dylan leaned toward Katie again and planted a long kiss on her lips.

~~~

Thank you so much for reading *Dylan*. If you enjoyed this book, I'd appreciate a review!

Lantern Beach Blackout: Danger Rising continues with *Maddox*. Get your copy HERE.
~~~

USA TODAY BESTSELLING AUTHOR
CHRISTY BARRITT
MADDOX
LANTERN BEACH
BLACKOUT

ALSO BY CHRISTY BARRITT:

OTHER BOOKS IN THE LANTERN BEACH SERIES:

LANTERN BEACH MYSTERIES

Hidden Currents

You can take the detective out of the investigation, but you can't take the investigator out of the detective. A notorious gang puts a bounty on Detective Cady Matthews's head after she takes down their leader, leaving her no choice but to hide until she can testify at trial. But her temporary home across the country on a remote North Carolina island isn't as peaceful as she initially thinks. Living under the new identity of Cassidy Livingston, she struggles to keep her investigative skills tucked away, especially after a body washes ashore. When local police bungle the murder investigation, she can't resist stepping in. But Cassidy is supposed to be keeping a low profile. One wrong move could lead to both her discovery and her demise. Can she bring justice to the island . . . or will the hidden currents surrounding her pull her under for good?

Flood Watch

The tide is high, and so is the danger on Lantern Beach. Still in hiding after infiltrating a dangerous gang, Cassidy Livingston just has to make it a few more months before she can testify at trial and resume her old life. But trouble keeps finding her, and Cassidy is pulled into a local investigation after a man mysteriously disappears from the island she now calls home. A recurring nightmare from her time undercover only muddies things, as does a visit from the parents of her handsome ex-Navy SEAL neighbor. When a friend's life is threatened, Cassidy must make choices that put her on the verge of blowing her cover. With a flood watch on her emotions and her life in a tangle, will Cassidy find the truth? Or will her past finally drown her?

Storm Surge

A storm is brewing hundreds of miles away, but its effects are devastating even from afar. Laid-back, loose, and light: that's Cassidy Livingston's new motto. But when a makeshift boat with a bloody cloth inside washes ashore near her oceanfront home, her detective instincts shift into gear . . . again. Seeking clues isn't the only thing on her mind—romance is heating up with next-door neighbor and former Navy SEAL Ty Chambers as well. Her heart wants the love and stability she's longed for her entire life. But her hidden identity only leads to a tidal wave of turbulence. As more answers emerge about the boat, the danger around her rises, creating a treacherous swell that threatens to reveal her past. Can Cassidy mind her own business, or will the storm surge of violence and corruption that has washed ashore on Lantern Beach leave her life in wreckage?

Dangerous Waters

Danger lurks on the horizon, leaving only two choices: find shelter or flee. Cassidy Livingston's new identity has begun to feel as comfortable as her favorite sweater. She's been tucked away on Lantern Beach for weeks, waiting to testify against a deadly gang, and is settling in to a new life she wants to last forever. When she thinks she spots someone malevolent from her past, panic swells inside her. If an enemy has found her, Cassidy won't be the only one who's a target. Everyone she's come to love will also be at risk. Dangerous waters threaten to pull her into an overpowering chasm she may never escape. Can

Cassidy survive what lies ahead? Or has the tide fatally turned against her?

Perilous Riptide

Just when the current seems safer, an unseen danger emerges and threatens to destroy everything. When Cassidy Livingston finds a journal hidden deep in the recesses of her ice cream truck, her curiosity kicks into high gear. Islanders suspect that Elsa, the journal's owner, didn't die accidentally. Her final entry indicates their suspicions might be correct and that what Elsa observed on her final night may have led to her demise. Against the advice of Ty Chambers, her former Navy SEAL boyfriend, Cassidy taps into her detective skills and hunts for answers. But her search only leads to a skeletal body and trouble for both of them. As helplessness threatens to drown her, Cassidy is desperate to turn back time. Can Cassidy find what she needs to navigate the perilous situation? Or will the riptide surrounding her threaten everyone and everything Cassidy loves?

Deadly Undertow

The current's fatal pull is powerful, but so is one detective's will to live. When someone from Cassidy Livingston's past shows up on Lantern Beach and warns her of impending peril, opposing currents collide, threatening to drag her under. Running would be easy. But leaving would break her heart. Cassidy must decipher between the truth and lies, between reality and deception. Even more importantly, she must decide whom to trust and whom to fear. Her life depends on it. As danger rises and answers surface, everything Cassidy thought she knew is tested. In order to survive, Cassidy must take drastic measures and end the battle against the ruthless gang DH-7 once and for all. But if her final mission fails, the consequences will be as deadly as the raging undertow.

LANTERN BEACH ROMANTIC SUSPENSE

Tides of Deception

Change has come to Lantern Beach: a new police chief, a new season, and . . . a new romance? Austin Brooks has loved Skye Lavinia from the moment they met, but the walls she keeps around her seem impenetrable. Skye knows Austin is the best thing to ever happen to her. Yet she also knows that if he learns the truth about her past, he'd be a fool not to run. A chance encounter brings secrets bubbling to the surface, and danger soon follows. Are the life-threatening events plaguing them really accidents . . . or is someone trying to send a deadly message? With the tides on Lantern Beach come deception and lies. One question remains—who will be swept away as the water shifts? And will it bring the end for Austin and Skye, or merely the beginning?

Shadow of Intrigue

For her entire life, Lisa Garth has felt like a supporting character in the drama of life. The designation never bothered her—until now. Lantern Beach, where she's settled and runs a popular restaurant, has boarded up for the season. The slower pace leaves her with too much time alone. Braden Dillinger came to Lantern Beach to try to heal. The former Special Forces officer returned from battle with invisible scars and diminished hope. But his recovery is hampered by the fact that an unknown enemy is trying to kill him. From the moment Lisa and Braden meet, danger ignites around them, and both are drawn into a web of intrigue that turns their lives upside down. As shadows creep in, will Lisa and Braden be able to shine a light on the peril around them? Or will the encroaching darkness turn their worst nightmares into reality?

Storm of Doubt

A pastor who's lost faith in God. A romance

writer who's lost faith in love. A faceless man with a deadly obsession. Nothing has felt right in Pastor Jack Wilson's world since his wife died two years ago. He hoped coming to Lantern Beach might help soothe the ragged edges of his soul. Instead, he feels more alone than ever. Novelist Juliette Grace came to the island to hide away. Though her professional life has never been better, her personal life has imploded. Her husband left her and a stalker's threats have grown more and more dangerous. When Jack saves Juliette from an attack, he sees the terror in her gaze and knows he must protect her. But when danger strikes again, will Jack be able to keep her safe? Or will the approaching storm prove too strong to withstand?

Winds of Danger

Wes O'Neill is perfectly content to hang with his friends and enjoy island life on Lantern Beach. Something begins to change inside him when Paige Henderson sweeps into his life. But the beautiful newcomer is hiding painful secrets beneath her cheerful facade. Police dispatcher Paige Henderson came to Lantern Beach riddled with guilt and uncertainties after the fallout of a bad relationship. When she meets Wes, she begins to open up to the possibility of love again. But there's something Wes isn't telling her—something that could change everything. As the winds shift, doubts seep into Paige's mind. Can Paige and Wes trust each other, even as the currents work against them? Or is trouble from the past too much to overcome?

Rains of Remorse

A stranger invades her home, leaving Rebecca Jarvis terrified. Above all, she must protect the baby growing inside her. Since her estranged husband died suspiciously six months earlier, Rebecca has been determined to depend on no one but herself. Her chivalrous new neighbor appears to be an answer to prayer. But who is Levi Stoneman really? Rebecca wants to believe he can help her, but she can't ignore her instincts. As danger closes in, both Rebecca and Levi must figure out whom they can trust. With Rebecca's baby coming soon, there's no time to waste. Can the truth prevail . . . or will remorse overpower the best of intentions?

Torrents of Fear

The woman lingering in the crowd can't be Allison . . . can she? Because Allison was pronounced dead six years ago. Musician Carter Denver knows only one person who's capable of helping him find answers: Sadie Thompson, his estranged best friend and someone who also knew Allison. He needs to know if he's losing his mind or if Allison could have survived her car accident. Could Allison really be alive? If so, why is she trying to harm Carter and Sadie? As the two try to find answers, can Sadie keep her feelings for Carter hidden? Could he ever care for her, or is the man of her dreams still in love with the woman now causing his nightmares?

LANTERN BEACH PD

On the Lookout

When Cassidy Chambers accepted the job as police chief on Lantern Beach, she knew the island had its secrets. But a suspicious death with potentially far-reaching implications will test all her skills—and threaten to reveal her true identity. Cassidy enlists the help of her husband, former Navy SEAL Ty Chambers. As they dig for answers, both uncover parts of their pasts that are best left buried. Not everything is as it seems, and they must figure out if their John Doe is connected to the secretive group that has moved onto the island. As facts materialize, danger on the island grows. Can Cassidy and Ty discover the truth about the shadowy crimes in their cozy community? Or has darkness permanently invaded their beloved Lantern Beach?

Attempt to Locate

A fun girls' night out turns into a nightmare when armed robbers barge into the store where Cassidy and her friends are shopping. As the situation escalates and the men escape, a massive manhunt launches on Lantern Beach to apprehend the dangerous trio. In the midst of the chaos, a potential foe asks for Cassidy's help. He needs to find his sister who fled from the secretive Gilead's Cove community on the island. But the more Cassidy learns about the seemingly untouchable group, the more her unease grows. The pressure to solve both cases continues to mount. But as the gravity of the situation rises, so does the danger. Cassidy is determined to protect the island and break up the cult . . . but doing so might cost her everything.

First Degree Murder

Police Chief Cassidy Chambers longs for a break from the recent crimes plaguing Lantern Beach. She simply wants to enjoy her friends' upcoming wedding, to prepare for the busy tourist season about to slam the island, and to gather all the dirt she can on the suspicious community that's invaded the town. But trouble explodes on the island, sending residents—including Cassidy—into a squall of uneasiness. Cassidy may have more than one enemy plotting her demise, and the collateral damage seems unthinkable. As the temperature rises, so does the pressure to find answers. Someone is determined that Lantern Beach would be better off without their new police chief. And for Cassidy, one wrong move could mean certain death.

Dead on Arrival

With a highly charged local election consuming the community, Police Chief Cassidy Chambers braces herself for a challenging day of breaking up petty conflicts and tamping down high emotions. But when widespread food poisoning spreads among potential voters across the island, Cassidy smells something rotten in the air. As Cassidy examines every possibility to uncover what's going on, local enigma Anthony Gilead again comes on her radar. The man is running for mayor and his cult-like following is growing at an alarming rate. Cassidy feels certain he has a spy embedded in her inner circle. The problem is that her pool of suspects gets deeper every day. Can Cassidy get to the bottom of what's eating away at her peaceful island home? Will voters turn out despite the outbreak of illness plaguing their tranquil town? And the even bigger question: Has darkness come to stay on Lantern Beach?

Plan of Action

A missing Navy SEAL. Danger at the boiling point. The ultimate showdown. When Police Chief Cassidy Chambers' husband, Ty, disappears, her world is turned upside down. His truck is discovered with blood inside, crashed in a ditch on Lantern Beach, but he's nowhere to be found. As they launch a manhunt to find him, Cassidy discovers that someone on the island has a deadly obsession with Ty. Meanwhile, Gilead's Cove seems to be imploding. As danger heightens, federal law enforcement officials are called in. The cult's growing threat could lead to the pinnacle standoff of good versus evil. A clear plan of action is needed or the results will be devastating. Will Cassidy find Ty in time, or will she face a gut-wrenching loss? Will Anthony Gilead finally be unmasked for who he really is and be brought to justice? Hundreds of innocent lives are at stake . . . and not everyone will come out alive.

LANTERN BEACH BLACKOUT

Dark Water

Colton Locke can't forget the black op that went terribly wrong. Desperate for a new start, he moves to Lantern Beach, North Carolina, and forms Blackout, a private security firm. Despite his hero status, he can't erase the mistakes he's made. For the past year, Elise Oliver hasn't been able to shake the feeling that there's more to her husband's death than she was told. When she finds a hidden box of his personal possessions, more questions—and suspicions—arise. The only person she trusts to help her is her husband's best friend, Colton Locke. Someone wants Elise dead. Is it because she knows too much? Or is it to keep her from finding the truth? The Blackout team must uncover dark secrets hiding beneath seemingly still waters. But those very secrets might just tear the team apart.

Safe Harbor

Guilt over past mistakes haunts former Navy SEAL Dez Rodriguez. When he's asked to guard a pop star during a music festival on Lantern Beach, he's all set for what he hopes is a breezy assignment. Bree hasn't found fame to be nearly as fulfilling as she dreamed. Instead, she's more like a carefully crafted character living out a pre-scripted story. When a stalker's threats become deadly, her life— and career—are turned upside down. From the start, Bree sees her temporary bodyguard as a player, and Dez sees Bree as a spoiled rich girl. But when they're thrown together in a fight for survival, both must learn to trust. Can Dez protect Bree—and his care-

fully guarded heart? Or will their safe harbor ulti-
mately become their death trap?

Ripple Effect

Griff McIntyre never expected his ex-wife and
three-year-old daughter to come to Lantern Beach.
After an abduction attempt, they're desperate for
safety. Now Griff's not letting either of them out of
his sight. Bethany knows Griff is the only one who
can protect them, despite the fact that he broke her
heart. But she'll do anything to keep her daughter
safe—even if it means playing nicely with a man she
can't stand. As peril ripples through their lives, Griff
and Bethany must work together to protect their
daughter. But an unseen enemy wants something
from them . . . and will stop at nothing to get it.
When disaster strikes, can Griff keep his family safe?
Or will past mistakes bring the ultimate failure?

Rising Tide

Benjamin James knows there's a traitor within his
former command. The rest of his team might even
think it's him. As danger closes in, he must clear
himself and stop a deadly plot by a dangerous
terrorist group. All CJ Compton wanted was a new
start after her career ended under suspicion. Working
as the house manager for private security group

Blackout seems perfect. But there's more trouble here than what she left behind. As the tide rushes in, the stakes continue to rise. If the Blackout team fails, it's not just Lantern Beach at stake—it's the whole country. Can Benjamin and CJ overcome their differences and work together to find the truth?

LANTERN BEACH BLACKOUT: THE NEW RECRUITS

Rocco

Former Navy SEAL and new Blackout recruit Rocco Foster is on a simple in and out mission. But the operation turns complicated when an unsuspecting woman wanders into the line of fire. Peyton Ellison's life mission is to sprinkle happiness on those around her. When a cupcake delivery turns into a fight for survival, she must trust her rescuer—a handsome stranger—to keep her safe. Rocco is determined to figure out why someone is targeting Peyton. First, he must keep the intriguing woman safe and earn her trust. But threats continue to pummel them as incriminating evidence emerges and pits them against each other. With time running out, the two must set aside both their growing attraction and their doubts about each other in order to work together. But the perilous facts they discover

leave them wondering what exactly the truth is . . .
and if the truth can be trusted.

Axel

*Women are missing. Private security firm Blackout
must find them before another victim disappears.* Axel
Hendrix likes to live on the edge. That's why being a
Navy SEAL suited him so well. But after his last
mission, he cut his losses and joined Blackout
instead. His team's latest case involves an undercover investigation on Lantern Beach. Olivia Rollins
came to the island to escape her problems—and
danger. When trouble from her past shows up in
town, she impulsively blurts she's engaged to Axel,
the womanizing man she's seen while waitressing.
Now, she may not be the only one in danger. So
could Axel. Axel knows Olivia might be his chance to
find answers and that acting like her fiancé is the
perfect cover for his latest assignment. But he doesn't
like throwing Olivia into the middle of such a
dangerous situation. Nor is he comfortable with the
feelings she stirs inside him. With Olivia's life—as
well as both their hearts—on the line, Axel must
uncover the truth and stop an evil plan before more
lives are destroyed.

Beckett

When the daughter of a federal judge is abducted, private security firm Blackout must find her. Psychologist Samantha Reynolds doesn't know why someone is targeting her. Even after a risky mission to save her, danger still lingers. She's determined to use her insights into the human mind to help decode the deadly clues being left in the wake of her rescue. Former Navy SEAL Beckett Jones needs to figure out who's responsible for the crimes hounding Sami. He's not sure why he's so protective of the woman he rescued, but he'll do anything to keep her safe—even if it means risking his heart. As the body count rises, there's no room for error. Beckett and Sami must both tear down the careful walls they've built around themselves in order to survive. If they don't figure out who's responsible, the madman will continue his death spree . . . and one of them might be next.

Gabe

When former Navy SEAL and current Blackout operative Gabe Michaels is almost killed in a hit-and-run, the aftermath completely upends his life. He's no longer safe—and he's not the only one. Dr. Autumn Spenser came to Lantern Beach to start fresh. But while treating Gabe after his accident, she senses there's more to what happened to him than meets the eye. When she digs deeper into his past, she never expects to be drawn into a deadly dilemma. Gabe has been infatuated with the pretty doctor since the day they met. Now, can he keep her from harm? Could someone out of his league ever return his feelings or will her past hurts keep them apart? As danger continues to pummel them, Gabe and Autumn are thrown together in a quest to find answers. More important than their growing attraction, they must stay alive long enough to stop the person desperate to destroy them.

LANTERN BEACH BLACKOUT: DANGER RISING

Brandon

Physically he's protecting her. But emotionally she's never felt more exposed. The last person tech heiress Finley Cooper ever wanted to see again was Brandon Hale. Two years ago, Brandon shattered her heart. Now Finley needs protection, and, against her wishes, Brandon is assigned the job. Even worse, they must pretend to be a couple in order to find answers. Brandon, a former Navy SEAL, met Finley while on an undercover assignment in Ecuador. But he broke her trust, and now he doesn't blame Finley for hating him. As a new Blackout operative, Brandon's first assignment throws him into Finley's life 24/7. Someone wants her dead, and it's clear this person won't stop until that mission is accomplished. To keep her safe, Brandon must regain Finley's trust. Can he convince her she's more than a job to him? Or will peril permanently silence them?

Dylan

His job is to protect her. The trouble is . . . she doesn't want protection. Former Navy SEAL Dylan Granger's new assignment requires him to use both his tactical abilities and his acting skills. Hired by Katie Logan's father, his job is to protect the gutsy university professor while concealing his identity. To maintain his cover, he takes the unassuming role of her new assistant. Katie—a disgraced reporter—has stumbled upon a lead she can't ignore. Now it's clear someone is targeting her, but she refuses to back down. Her handsome new assistant is a welcome distraction from the chaos. But Dylan's skillset goes way beyond his job description, and Katie begins to suspect there's more to Dylan than he's letting on. Dylan's mission can't be disclosed—not if he wants to keep Katie safe. But as his feelings for her grow and the danger increases, keeping his secret becomes more of a challenge than he ever imagined. With innocent lives on the line, Dylan must choose between protecting Katie or saving others.

LANTERN BEACH MAYDAY

Run Aground

A dead captain on a luxury yacht leads to a tumultuous seafaring journey . . . Med student Kenzie Anderson, tired of letting others chart her future, accepts a job as second steward aboard *Almost Paradise*. But when she finds the captain dead before the charter even begins, her plans seem to capsize. Jimmy James Gamble senses something vulnerable and slightly naive about Kenzie when he finds her on the docks. Realizing danger may still be lingering close, he uses his hidden skills to earn a place on the charter. But being there causes him to risk everything —especially as more suspicious incidents occur. As they set out to sea, Kenzie and Jimmy James both wonder if they're in over their heads. They must figure out how to stop a killer before anyone onboard is hurt . . . otherwise, both their futures might just run aground.

Dead Reckoning

A yachtie fears for her life when she's the only witness to a murder . . . Kenzie Anderson knows what she saw at the harbor—a woman strangled and pushed overboard. But there's no proof of a crime . . . only her word. Jimmy James Gamble believes Kenzie, even if no one else does. As he senses the danger in the air, all he wants is to keep her away from any more trouble—especially after their last charter. Either Kenzie or the yacht they're working on seem to be a magnet for murder and mayhem. Someone is willing to kill to get what he wants—and will do so again if necessary. Can Jimmy James and Kenzie navigate these unfamiliar waters? Or will relying on dead reckoning lead them to their deaths?

Tipping Point

Awakening in a boat surrounded by nothing but water, a yachtie has no doubt someone wants her dead. Kenzie Anderson is determined not to let anyone scare her away from completing the charter season—even with the threats on her life. The only person she can trust is Captain Jimmy James Gamble, despite their tumultuous relationship. Kenzie and Jimmy James both suspect turbulent currents rush beneath the tranquil surface aboard the luxury yacht *Almost Paradise*. Secrets seem to abound, each one increasing the tension aboard the boat. As answers rise to the surface, neither Kenzie nor Jimmy James is prepared for what they find. Have they both reached their tipping points? Their adversaries want nothing more than to make Kenzie disappear . . . forever. It may be too late for a mayday call.

ABOUT THE AUTHOR

USA Today has called Christy Barritt's books "scary, funny, passionate, and quirky."

Christy writes both mystery and romantic suspense novels that are clean with underlying messages of faith. Her books have won the Daphne du Maurier Award for Excellence in Suspense and Mystery, have been twice nominated for the Romantic Times Reviewers' Choice Award, and have finaled for both a Carol Award and Foreword Magazine's Book of the Year.

She is married to her Prince Charming, a man who thinks she's hilarious—but only when she's not trying to be. Christy is a self-proclaimed klutz, an avid music lover who's known for spontaneously bursting into song, and a road trip aficionado.

When she's not working or spending time with her family, she enjoys singing, playing the guitar, and exploring small, unsuspecting towns where people have no idea how accident-prone she is.

Find Christy online at:
www.christybarritt.com
www.facebook.com/christybarritt
www.twitter.com/cbarritt

Sign up for Christy's newsletter to get information on all of her latest releases here: **www.christybarritt. com/newsletter-sign-up/**